Shimmer

Shimmer

Cas K

Shimmer
By Cas K

Haley was sitting in her parked car in the driveway of her house. She wasn't nervous about going into the house, no, she was *reeling* from the day she just went through. Her anxiety had gotten the best of her one too many times and then her manager yelled at her for taking a break to deal with her anxiety attacks. She took deep breaths and ran a hand through her blonde hair. The day was over, and she could stop worrying about it. Nicole, her roommate and best friend, had a date and that meant she had the house to herself for a couple of hours. Which also meant catching up on tv. A small smile appeared on her pale face; she couldn't wait to get caught up on her favorite show. The show was about a woman superhero who had worked hard to make a name for herself. She brought herself back to reality and took a few more calming breaths. Haley then got out of her car and went to the front door. She took one more deep breath, there was no need to bring the day with her. She reminded herself to leave work at work. Then, she finally headed inside, ready to unwind from the day.

"Hey, Hal," Nicole greeted cheerily as soon as Haley walked through the door. Nicole was the first to call Haley 'Hal' and Hal loved it, she thought it was sweet. Nicole was on the couch in the living room that was overseen by the kitchen and dining room. Haley took a deep breath in; she loved the sweet vanilla and peppermint scent that filled the house. They always had a wax warmer with a scent matching the season. It was a small tradition for them, when the season changed so did the scent in the house. Although sometimes they would have a stress relief scent too if they were having a rough day.

"Thought you had a date?" Hal asked as she set her stuff down and set her keys into the key dish. She shrugged off her coat and set it on the catch all chair. She mentally reminded herself to clean that up later.

"Not for another hour," Nicole replied, giving her a raised brow. Nicole then went back to scrolling through her phone. Hal could tell she was nervous about this date. She could tell by the way Nicole had her arm over her stomach and how her leg was bouncing lightly.

"Right, forgot," Hal said while snapping a finger gun in return. Hal's blue eyes gazed over Nicole and admired how Nicole's brown hair fell onto her shoulders in waves. She sat with one foot under her and a blanket on her lap. She had on a black t-shirt and jeans. Even in the simplest outfit, Nicole looked gorgeous.

Without taking her brown eyes off of her phone, Nicole gestured to the dining room table, "A package came for you today, it's on the table."

"I don't re- I didn't order anything," Hal said to herself as she picked up the package and took it to the kitchen. She grabbed a knife from a drawer and opened the box. There was only a rose gold band in it. Not even a letter or a receipt. She took the box to her room, figuring it was a mix-up.

She set the box on her dresser and started to change out of her work clothes. She changed into her favorite crewneck sweatshirt and a pair of leggings. As she brushed her hair and paced, thoughts of work began to bother her brain. Then, she began to feel a familiar tightness in her chest. She stopped what she was doing and started taking deep breaths. She could feel that familiar fear as it flared up as it always does when work is on her mind. So, she started her calm-down routine. Her calm-down routine consisted of going through her senses. Five things she can see, four things she can touch, three things she could hear, two things she could smell, and one thing she could taste. So, pointed out five things in her room, then went and touched four of those things. Then, she listened for three different things, traffic, the music Nicole had playing, and her ceiling fan. Finally, she pointed out the wax warmer in the main section of the house and then the air plug in that was in her room. She lastly grabbed a mint from her tin on her nightstand. After all that, she felt better. She hated panic attacks, but with her occasional medicine calm-down routine she was able to keep them in check.

Now that she was calmer, she could focus on the package that came for her. She picked it up and double checked the shipping label. It *was* addressed to her. However, she didn't find a return label.

"Okay," Hal said to herself, "either you have a *really* creepy secret admirer, or this is a prank from Nicole or another friend... Or something nice too."

She picked up the rose gold band and inspected it. The band wasn't too fancy, and it was big enough to be a headband. Her brows furrowed; she couldn't think of the last time she wore a headband. It was probably when she was a kid in elementary school. Subconsciously, she sat down on her bed and kept staring at it then drifted off into other thoughts. Random thoughts, like about the cute guy at work, who was also her friend, and how she wished she had the confidence to ask him-

"Hal?" Nicole knocked on the door before opening it. Hal hid the band behind her, and Nicole spoke as she opened the door, "I'm heading out to my date now." Nicole noticed how her friend was slightly slouched over and the sad look on her face. Nicole sat next to Hal, "You okay?"

Hal looked at Nicole and faked a smile. Hal then spoke, "Yeah, I'm fine. Go have fun on your date and if anything goes south text me the secret word and I'll call you. What should the emergency be in case?"

"Something happened and you need to go to the ER?" She asked. Hal nodded. Nicole continued, "Sounds good. Are you sure you're okay? Did you have a panic attack?"

"Yeah," Hal let out a small breath, "But it's fine. *I'm fine.* I'm just gonna watch some TV."

"Alright," Nicole replied, backing off the topic.

The two shared a hug before Nicole left for the night. As soon as Nicole was gone, Hal let out a sigh of relief. She loved having her friend's support but sometimes she just wanted to be left alone. She grabbed the band from behind her and lay back on her bed. Then, she examined the band again. She looked closely at it in hopes that there was an inscription on it. There was no such luck, unfortunately.

I'm so glad that got to you, a voice said. Hal sat up in a panic. She couldn't tell if that voice was out loud or in her head. It was just too damn quiet in the house to tell.

"Uh, who's there?" Hal stood up and reached for the bat she kept in her room. The bat was from when her and her friends tried softball, but it didn't work out for them.

Yeah, the bat is not going to work. I'm communicating with you telepathically. As in through your-
"I know what that is," Hal cut the voice off. "Who are you?"

My name is Roman. I come from the future, Roman told her. His voice was low, and he had an American accent. Roman continued when she didn't respond, *I had the rose gold band delivered to you because-*

"How far in the future?" Hal interrupted him again. She felt bad for interrupting him, but she was so curious about him. She wanted to know more about him and the time he came from.

What- I'm from the year 3045. Can we please stay on topic?

"Yeah," Hal let out a small sigh, "continue."

Haley Parker, I come from the year thirty-forty-five. In the future, many innocent lives have been lost to Esimed. After the latest fight against him, I was able to track him through time and he's now here. We don't know why exactly but the woman who not only invented that band but also wore it, was a hero and tasked me to bring it back here to you and ask you to-

"I'm in." Hal replied with a smile on her face. To her it sounded like a chance to be a superhero and she was *so* in.

Just like that? I didn't even tell you the risks-

"So? It sounds like you're asking me to be a superhero-"

I am.

"Well, I *love* superheroes. I want to be like them, and this is my chance, I'll do it," Hal said confidently. Hal already knew the risks, it's the same with every superhero.

Thank you. First, you need to put on the band so that it sits on your forehead.

"Okay?" She asked as she picked up the band again.

Hal put the band on her forehead then looked at herself in the mirror. Rose gold was one of her favorites and *it looked cool,* but nothing was happening. She opened her mouth to say something when suddenly this shimmering white, blue light started rising in a circle around her. It moved like water around her and circled around her legs first. Changing her into thigh high black boots. Then, it moved up her legs and then around her torso turning her clothes into this blue velvet, long sleeve, legless bodysuit. Then, the shimmering light moved and spread into an almost floor length cape shape on her back and made a white cape in its wake. Then, the shimmering water-like stuff vanished. Hal went over to her full-sized mirror. She was shocked. Then, she noticed her very pure white cape and smiled. She loved capes. She spun around with her cape and admired the way it twirled around her and shimmered in the light. Then, she looked at the deep blue bodysuit and thigh high boots. She felt a little self-conscious in the legless bodysuit because she was plus sized. She tried to push down her insecurities since there were more important matters at hand.

"Uh, Roman?" She began, "Does the guy's version also look like this?"

Yes. This band was intended for women that hold the same DNA as you. It technically isn't compatible with men. Why?

"Oh, I was just wondering," she said as she continued to admire herself in the mirror. She then blinked and remembered what he said earlier, "What do you mean by women that hold the same DNA as me?"

Well, the band was designed by your great-great-great granddaughter. She wanted the band to only work for the women in her family as a safety precaution.

"My-? My great-great-great *granddaughter*?" Hal's eyes went wide. She could feel tears starting to pool in her eyes. She never thought that she would have a family in that sense. She quickly calmed herself down before she was a blubbering mess.

Yes? Roman said, unsure of why she was shocked at the news of her having a bloodline.

"So, what powers do I have? Am I like a magical girl? Or an alien superhero? Or a goddess superhero? Or-"
No, but I do know that you can use magic-

"Oh! Like a sorcerer?"

Basically. You can cast spells that don't directly affect you. Your constant powers are super strength, flight, and energy beams with lighting that come out of your hands.

"So, do I have *any* weaknesses?" Hal asked.

Sort of. You can cast the wrong spell or not even cast a spell and you're not indestructible. Does that make sense?

Hal let out a breath she didn't realize she was holding. So, all she had to do was remember to cast the spell. Like that wasn't hard. She started pacing. She knew how bad she could forget things. What if she forgot to cast a spell and that cost her someone's life? She started to spiral down the anxiety hole.

Haley? Roman picked up on her emotions and attempted to get her attention. *Haley?*

"Makes sense," she responded. She was still scared of what *could* happen. "So, I'm still vulnerable if I don't cast the right spell, sounds easy. *How* do I cast a spell?"

Well, you don't speak. From what I've been told, you feel the spell and make movements to match. The inventor and previous owner told me that's what she did. The band would in turn pick up on these changes in you and help you put out the spell.

Just as they were about to delve deeper, Hal's phone started getting a bunch of texts from Nicole. Hal froze.

"Am I bulletproof?" She asked blankly.

Yes, the inventor made sure to include that in your constant powers.

Hal ran out the front door. Once she was clear, she took off to her friend. She flew quickly and if it weren't for the emergency, she would've been enjoying the feeling of flying. Once she arrived at the concert venue she came to a halt. She didn't want to cause any property damage, but people were in danger. So, she quickly decided to fly through the roof. She landed next to the gunman, and in a superhero pose by accident. The gunman looked at her in shock and started firing at her. Hal flipped her hair out of her face and stood to face the gunman.

The gunman's eyes widened, and he shot her a couple more times. The flattened bullets fell to the ground, tinging when they met the wooden stage. Hal looked up from her chest and looked at him. Fear was written all over his face. She took a step forward and grabbed the barrel of the gun.

She pulled the gun out of the way and punched the man in the face. He stumbled back, clutching his nose. She broke the gun on her knee. Her hands moved as if she was wrapping a rope around her hands. He came after her and she blocked his punch using the glowing rope that appeared in her hands. She moved her one hand so that his hand was trapped in the rope. She then swiftly got the other hand in the rope and tied him up.

Then, she faced the crowd. All of them had their phones out, still processing the shock they all felt. A silence had fallen over the crowd. Hal's eyes searched for Nicole among the crowd. At first when she couldn't find her, she panicked. Just as the worst thoughts came, they instantly disappeared when her eyes landed on her friend.

"Are there anymore?" She gently asked the crowd. A unanimous no filled the room. "Okay, everyone, let me get the bad guy and you follow me out, okay?"

Thankfully they listened to her and let her go first with the bad guy. She dragged him out to the cops as she floated her way out. When she got to the door, she set the bad guy down and slowly opened the door.

"Please don't shoot!" she yelled out, "I have the gunman!"

"Then come out slowly! We're coming to you for the shooter!" One cop said over the horn. She did as they asked, and they all looked shocked to see her. Most likely because she was still floating. She handed the shooter over to them.

The one cop spoke, "Are there..." he trailed off not knowing how to word it.

"The people are behind me and would like to come out," she replied as she set herself back on the ground. He nodded and they started letting them out. Almost everyone thanked her on their way out. Nicole didn't because she was on her phone, texting Hal. Hal looked away from Nicole and to the woman who came up to her.

"Excuse me?" She shyly asked.

"What's up?" Hal responded. She immediately regretted her word choice. Superheroes don't say 'what's up.'

"Uh, can I... get a picture with you?"

She smiled and nodded, "Of course!"

They posed and soon more came up and were talking to her, asking for photos, and hugs. Some cried and thanked her while others just shook her hand. One came up with their phone recording and asked her the infamous question, "Who are you?"

"Uh," She thought. She then heard a kid mentioned how her cape shimmered. Then, she spoke, "Shimmer."

"Thank you, Shimmer." The person smiled and walked away. Hal hoped that name wouldn't come back to bite her in the rear.

"You're welcome." Shimmer had her hands on her hips subconsciously, the classic superhero pose.

Shimmer said her last few words before taking off back to the house she shared with Nicole. As she flew back, adrenaline rushed through her veins. She had just saved Nicole and others. She couldn't help the grin on her face.

She landed and quickly took off the band so she could look like herself. She walked up to the townhouse she shared with her roommate and turned on the tv to the local news. She *really* hoped to see news about her. The news was still on commercial break when she tuned in. She set the band in her room before going to sit on the couch. Suddenly, the door opened, and it was Nicole, who was pretty shaken up. Hal stood and waited for Nicole to come over. They met in the middle and hugged. Hal whispered that it was okay and other reassuring words to calm down Nicole.

Nicole pulled away, still lingering in Hal's arms, and spoke, "Hal, you'll never believe this, there was a real-life superhero! She saved our lives. I didn't get to meet her; I had to come home and see you."

"That's amazing, I'm so glad you're safe," Hal replied with a smile. The news came back from break. They fully let go of each other and sat to watch the news.

"This just in, there was a shooting at a local concert tonight. Only four were injured. Of course, this could've been much worse if it weren't for Arizona's real-life superhero. Some are calling her a miracle. We go live now to Paul, who's spoken with the victims. Paul."

"Thank you, Allie. From what was a night of fun turned to a night of horror and then a miracle, victims are thankful for this superhero named Shimmer. Eyewitnesses say she took the shooter down in one fell swoop."

The screen cut to a victim, the one Hal got a selfie with, "It was crazy! At first, we were waiting for the main act to come on and this guy shows up and starts shooting. He stopped when he heard the cops.

Then, Shimmer came in and took him down! After, she let me thank her and take a picture with her!"

Then, it did a little montage of the victims and their statements, "I still can't believe it. I thought we were goners."

"I am so grateful she showed up, I was terrified."

"My daughter and I are forever in debt to her."

"If she's watching, I just want to say thank you. You saved us."

It cut back to Paul, "As you can see many are thankful for this superhero called Shimmer."

Then, they showed cell phone footage and pictures of Shimmer that others had gotten. They showed her showing up and taking down the shooter and the thank you videos. Luckily Nicole didn't recognize her as Shimmer.

"I told you, Hal!" Nicole smiled and then lit up with an idea, "Maybe you can help Shimmer!"

Hal smiled, "Yeah, that'd be awesome! I hope we get to see more of her."

"Maybe!" Nicole said before she yawned, "Well, that was a lot for me tonight, I'm gonna try to sleep. Good night."

Hal set a hand on Nicole's thigh and looked into her eyes, "You sure you're okay? You went through a lot."

Nicole placed her hand atop Hal's and spoke gently, "I know but seeing Shimmer was incredible and I'm so thankful for her. I'll take off work tomorrow so I can regain myself, okay?"

Hal bit her lip, "Okay. If you need-"

"I will let you know," Nicole patted her hand and got up, "good night, Hal."

Nicole headed off to bed and once Hal heard the door shut, she excitedly stood up. Hal was thrilled. She continued to watch the coverage of her. It was all very exciting; she didn't ever think that her first time out would go this well.

You can't tell anyone that you're Shimmer. Roman broke the silence, scaring the crap out of Hal.

"Why not?" Hal asked. She wanted to tell Nicole more than anything.

It's dangerous.

-

A man walked through a portal in an alleyway somewhere in the city. He wore an all-black cloak; the hood hid most of his face. He walked out to the sidewalk and took in his surroundings. He walked down the street until he saw a tv store with the news currently broadcasting a breaking story about the new hero known as Shimmer. He observed the footage of Shimmer, he could tell she was new just by how she held herself. He tilted his head when he realized how familiar she looked to him. She was wearing the same band and outfit as his previous foe but that didn't mean anything. And it didn't matter if he knew her or not, he had to take her out in order for his plan to succeed.

He huffed out a breath and continued walking. He found a construction site and decided to hide out there for now. He had to find the sunset stone before anyone knew he was here.

-

3

Hal woke up the next morning still in shock from last night. She felt like she was hungover but in a good way, like she was still happy. It all felt like a dream. As she got ready for work, she wondered if any of her friends knew about Shimmer yet. She was sure some people knew by now. She thought it would be so cool to be known like that. Even though no one would *know* it's her. Maybe keeping it a secret wouldn't be so bad after all.

However, Nicole was her best friend. Her mind then rattled on about *how* it was dangerous to tell Nicole that she was Shimmer. Wouldn't it be safer to tell her? So that when suddenly she's gone and Shimmer shows up, Nicole doesn't have to worry. And it *would* build their trust with each other. She wouldn't have to lie or feel like she was lying. And she'd only tell Nicole.

Hal let out a sigh, she had to keep it secret. She knew it would make her life easier. Hal finished getting ready before heading out of her room and into the kitchen.

"Morning, Hal!" Nicole greeted her with a smile. She was sitting at the dining room table, sipping tea and eating breakfast. Even if Nicole was putting on a brave and chipper face, Hal could tell that Nicole was faking it. Hal could see the fear that still lingered in her eyes. She saw it last night but didn't want to press further and upset her friend.

Hal raised an eyebrow, "Why are you so chipper?"

"Well," Nicole stood up and made her way to Hal, "people are still talking about Shimmer and, honestly, without her, I think I'd be dead. I'm just so grateful, Hal."

"Oh, makes sense," Hal said slowly the turned to get food, "we still have French toast?"

"Yes, we do because we had leftovers from Sunday brunch. You always make too much for brunch," Nicole replied as she went back to her seat at the table. Hal then went to get her breakfast.

Nicole was right, if it weren't for Shimmer, she'd be dead. It was a grim thought, but Hal was grateful for getting that band. She would've lost her best friend if she never got it. Hal wouldn't know what to do without Nicole. She was her rock and was always there for her no matter what it was. Hal loved her spark, her kindness, and Nicole always looked on the bright side. Nicole was someone that Hal trusted with her life, and it killed her that she couldn't talk to her about being Shimmer. Hal glanced at her watch and finished her breakfast and cleaned up.

"Are you staying home today?" Hal asked as she walked over to the door. Nicole nodded and walked over to her. They shared a hug and a few goodbyes before Hal left for work.

Eventually, Hal made it to work and was already getting a panic attack. Luckily, she made it a little early to do one of her calm-down routines. After some breathing and positive affirmations, she calmed down again. She also told herself calming words that Nicole tells her after a panic attack. She then took a deep breath and walked in to get to her desk and smiled when she saw her co-worker and friend, Ariana, waiting for her.

Ariana was the same size as and height as Hal with straight dark brown hair and wore black rimmed glasses for her hazel eyes. She was always enthusiastic for her friends. Basically, she was the hype man of the group. On weekends, she volunteered at the animal shelter. She had a big heart and was definitely the type of girl to put everyone before her. She had so much love to give and only a few people returned it, which was also her downfall. Her boyfriend would take advantage of her kindness and big heart. She would show up with bruises on her arms but never mentioned it to anyone even though deep down she was hurting. Ariana was good at hiding her pain. Nicole tried to convince Ariana to leave her boyfriend, but she was against it. Nicole and Hal understood, so they offered to protect her when she needed it.

"Hey, girl!" Ariana greeted, "Did you see the news?"

"Yeah?" Hal answered with a raised brow.

"Dude! There was a real-life superhero! I'm shocked you're not freaking out!" Ariana said excitedly. Hal gave her a small brief smile.

"Sorry, Nicole was there, it was a long night."

"Oh my gosh, I'm so sorry. Is she-?"

"She survived, thankfully. I think if it weren't for that superhero she wouldn't be here."

"Is she okay, though?" Ariana made direct eye contact with her. Hal looked away then, set her stuff down and got her desk set up and clocked in.

"She's shaken up but grateful for- what was the superhero's name?"

"Oh, Shimmer. Interesting name."

"Yeah." Hal hid the fact that she couldn't tell if she loved or hated the name she chose. The two talked a little more until their manager came over.

"Ladies," Linda started, "you need to be on the phone."

Linda was their manager and team leader of the small group. She wasn't the best either. Hal knew she wanted the best team, but Hal had panic attacks. They met on multiple occasions about her mental health. Linda said something along the lines of 'just plan around it and within your allotted time.' Linda wasn't the most empathetic person and it showed. She always told Hal to just deal with her panic attacks, that they were nothing and easy to get rid of. Then, Linda wanted a list of all the times Hal was not on the phone. Hal did the list and Linda still got upset because apparently a panic attack isn't something that should be put on there. Hal felt like she was stuck between a rock and a hard place with her.

They nodded and got to work. It felt like *ages* until lunch made its way around. Hal was starving and excited to see Chris, her crush *and* friend. She hoped he liked Shimmer. She wouldn't know what to do if he didn't. She figured she'd have to convince him to like Shimmer. But, if he was truly adamant about not liking Shimmer, she'd have to accept it and move on. She sent up a silent prayer that he did like Shimmer. She finished up her last call and clocked out for lunch.

After getting food, she sat down with friends and across from Chris. Chris had auburn hair that was a little disheveled but in a neat way. He had kind hazel eyes and a bit of stubble on his strong jaw that Hal loved. He was also taller than Hal and very muscular. Hal and Chris were pretty good friends and had been for quite some time. Ariana introduced them and they found out that they were into a lot of the same things. When it's just them they can talk forever, and Hal loved that. She loved how he would lean in when he was getting more interested in the topic at hand or how he smiled and laughed at their dumb jokes. He was such a sweet and kind person. She had fallen for this guy, and she couldn't help the small smile that appeared on her face when she thought of him. She shook off the smile and listened to the group talk about their recent calls and hoped someone would bring up Shimmer.

"So," Jeff, one of Hal's least favorite people, started, "did you guys see about this Shimmer girl last night?"

"Yeah," Ariana gushed, "I think it's so cool we get a real-life superhero!"

"She is pretty cool," Chris commented, "I hope we get to see her again. What do you think, Hal?"

"I think she's awesome and I'm so grateful for her. If she didn't exist, I don't think Nicole would be here," Hal gave a small smile. She was so happy that Chris liked Shimmer so far.

"Nicole was there?" Jeff asked with concern. Sure, Jeff was concerned but that's because he had a thing for Nicole. He was always flirting with her and making advances towards her. Nicole would always reject him. He did ask her out a few times and Nicole declined each one. Which was fair, Jeff was the type of dude who thought he was better by putting others down. He would sometimes insult Hal on her weight and Hal at first would retort with some witty comeback, but she just flat out ignores him. He never commented on Nicole's weight, though. Which was kind of upsetting at first, but Hal got over it. Hal was confident in herself and didn't need someone like Jeff to bring her down.

"Yeah, she's just shaken up and decided to stay home today," Hal replied gently. She didn't want to talk to Jeff about Nicole's condition. It wasn't her place, either.

"That's good," Jeff said, "Back to Shimmer. Why would she show up now? What about past events? Why now?"

"See, I agree," Tyler started, "who is she and why now?"

Tyler was the group's friend first. Then, he met Jeff. Somehow, Tyler became Jeff's right hand man in the weirdest way, and it was weird for everyone. Tyler was always the one to jump on board with Jeff. They all tried to convince Tyler to leave Jeff in the friend sense. Tyler argued that Jeff is a great guy, and that they have to get to know him. So, they put up with Jeff for Tyler's sake. And to see if Jeff ever stopped being an asshole and so far, he hasn't stopped.

The two kept slandering Shimmer and Hal couldn't take it, so she spoke up, "Maybe she *just now* got her powers. She's probably wanted to help this *whole* time but never could and now she can. I believe that she's going to be here for us. No matter what."

"Still," Jeff continued with a look of disgust on his pale and freckled face, "our first superhero is *fat*?"

"Right! I wish she were hotter," Tyler said. He shook his brown hair out of his face.

Hal glared at them. He always brought up women's weights and it was getting annoying. Jeff was a big guy, so Hal didn't see why he felt the need to bring it up. Hal looked away from Jeff and Tyler and to her lunch. It didn't look appetizing anymore. She let out a small sigh and rolled her eyes.

"Seriously, Jeff?" Chris started, "Shimmer kicks ass, that's more than what you can do."

"And," Ariana continued, "you're just as big if not bigger, you have no right to talk like that."

Jeff scoffed and walked off muttering how he had to get back to work anyway. Tyler quickly joined Jeff. Hal had a feeling that the two were still going to talk down about Shimmer. The rest talked a bit more about Shimmer. They mentioned all the good things how they were excited to see what Shimmer would do next. Hal kept focusing on her breathing, trying to calm herself. She loved hearing the love from her friends about her secret identity. However, Jeff and Tyler really peeved her. She hated that they talked about her, Shimmer, like that. She had to calm down before she went back to the phone. So, before lunch ended, she went to the courtyard that's never visited and sat on a bench underneath a tree.

What they said was awful, but I believe in you. Roman told her once she was alone.

"Thanks, Roman." She replied. Then, a thought came to her mind, "Where are you?"

What? Roman asked. She was very curious as to where he was. Hell, she thought maybe this was all a fever dream, too.

"Well," she started, "I *assume* you're in some kind of spaceship and that maybe you're orbiting in space?"

I am on a ship. Why do you ask?

She shrugged, "Dunno. Curious, I guess."

Well, if you want to know, I am not in orbit. I'm just hidden some-where here in Arizona. Middle of nowhere.

"So, then why can't we talk in person?" She asked. He never outright said they could never talk in person, but it felt like it.

Because Esimed could find me, and I don't want to fight him or put you in more danger.

"So, you're scared?"

No-no, I'm not. It's mostly to protect you.

"Sounds like you are." Hal said as she leaned back on the bench. She then thought about how dangerous this Esimed could be if someone that's already fought him is scared of him. Roman went silent after that. Hal then thought of another question, her voice was gentle as she spoke, "What did Esimed do?"

Roman was hesitant at first but he answered, *For many years he wreaked havoc and destroyed so many lives. He was ruthless, he didn't care who died. He only cares about getting what he wants.*

"Why is he like that?" Hal raised a brow.

In the future, we found out that Esimed had a great life and had great parents, but he was just... evil. We couldn't find anything that set him off. The woman, Eliana, who wore that band before you, tried to take him down but she ultimately failed.

"Is the woman-?" Hal asked.

The point is, Esimed is dangerous. I'm sorry, I can't talk about her to you.

Hal decided not to press on the matter further and to get back to work. The rest of the day was normal and finally, she got to clock out. Freedom and homebound. However, Hal was concerned about her conversation with Roman from earlier. Why was he so scared? How bad was this threat? And who was Elliana to him? She had a lot of questions that only Roman could answer.

Hal was sitting in her car in the driveway again after work. She was *still* upset over lunch. She could believe that Jeff and Tyler would say those things, but it still hurt. She was tearing up because she knew there were more people who thought the same as him too. She let out a breath and wiped away her tears. She didn't want Nicole to know she was crying about a dumb comment. Also, it was about Shimmer and one thing could lead to another and Nicole would know. So, it was time to calm down. Once she calmed down and adjusted her makeup, she went inside.

"I'm home," Hal called out as she closed and locked the door. She took off her jacket and set it on the catch all chair. There was no response, so she called out again, "Nini?"

Hal raised a brow and went to Nicole's room. She knocked on the door gently; when there was no response, she opened the door and saw Nicole sleeping on the bed. Hal let out a sigh of relief and then went to her office.

Her office not only held her computer stuff but her sewing supplies. Nicole had a painting office that she loved very much. Hal and Nicole loved their little offices. It was their place to escape from everything. Hal shut the door and set her bag down. She then grabbed the rose gold band and held it. She had to talk to Roman, she wanted to train, go out and fight crime, *anything*.

"Roman," she gently spoke out, "I want to do more. *Please.*"

Silence. She waited for what felt like forever and never got a response. He was gone. She started to think this was all a dream. There was no way she was this lucky and besides, no one like her would get this opportunity. She started to feel her throat close up and tears prick at her eyes. She quickly wiped them away, she had to be wrong. She huffed out a sigh. Or maybe he changed his mind about her. Either way, she figured it was on her. Which made her want to cry more.

So, she turned on a live stream of the news, hoping for a chance to be Shimmer again. The news went on about how temperatures have been low, then about how a local business helped kids in need and so on. Before Hal could zone out, it cut to breaking news. There was a fire at a local grocery store. Hal stood, got the information she needed before transforming and heading out.

She floated a couple miles above the store. She had to think. How could she put this out? Then it hit her. She brought a fist to her lips before blowing the air in her fist away, almost like blowing a kiss and that created cold air. She swooped down to the flames. One of the firefighters grabbed her attention and she went over to him.

"Shimmer, thank God!" The firefighter captain said. She gave him a smile and a nod.

"Are there any civilians inside?" She asked.

He shook his head and she rose back up in the air. She started blowing cold air onto the fires. She had to maneuver in a way that was almost difficult for her. She would fly up then down, then close, then far and she had to do this until all the fire was out. It felt like a solid hour before it was all out. She quickly went through the rubble, putting out any other flames making sure it was all out. She also double checked for people, just in case. Once she was done, she met back with the firefighter captain.

"Thank you, Shimmer, thank you," he said as Hal shook his hand. Then, people surrounded her. They started asking for pictures, hugs, and offering simple thank yous. Hal couldn't help the smile that formed on her lips. It was such a rush being Shimmer and interacting with the public after was a whole new feeling.

"Shimmer!" One woman shouted as she came up with her cell phone, recording.

Shimmer spun around to meet the woman, "Yes, ma'am?"

"You haven't been here long but have already done so much for the community, how can we repay you?" The woman asked. She didn't look like she was a victim of the fire. She was dressed business casual and seemed very familiar.

"Thank you," Shimmer started, "I just really appreciate your support and hope that I can continue to help the community."

"One more question," she pleaded. Shimmer nodded. The woman smiled, "Are we going to find out who you really are?"

Shimmer had a grin on her face, "Well, that's my secret. If any-one knew who I was, everyone I know would be in danger." Shimmer glanced at the sky as she heard sirens in the distance, "Well, that's my cue. Thank you and have a good day!"

Shimmer took off to the next emergency. It was a home invasion. She helped the police to bring the criminals out and into custody. The police and family thanked her, Hal thanked them for her support before taking off again.

She then landed in the backyard of her house and took off the band. She then went back inside. She checked on Nicole, who was still sleeping, and then went about eating dinner, checking the news for Shimmer, and finally heading to bed.

-

4

Two days later and still nothing from Roman. Hal was frustrated about it the day before but got over it the next day. She didn't want to get too angry; it wasn't good for her health. Hal shook off the thoughts and tried to focus on something else. She had been off work and was in her office. She had her legs propped up on her desk and was balancing a pencil on her upper lip. She was procrastinating. Sure, she could be working on her hobbies, but she was not motivated to do anything but balance a pencil.

I see you've been busy. Roman's voice came through, scaring the shit out of Hal causing her to nearly fall out of her chair.

"I could say the same to you," she paused, "I'm sorry if I upset you the other day. Where have you been?" Hal replied, fixing herself and setting the pencil on the desk. She leaned back in her chair and folded her hands on her stomach.

You didn't upset me; I've been researching Esimed. I know he's in this year, but I can't seem to find out why or where exactly.

"Maybe we could track him down and ask him?" Hal asked, semi-serious. She then leaned forward in her chair and pulled out her phone, "Anyway, people have been talking about me. It's so cool and-"

We can do that. Roman interrupted.

"Excuse me? Do what?"

Track him down and ask him. All you need is some training. You in?

"I'm *so* in." Hal grabbed the band and put it in her bag. She then slipped on some shoes before grabbing her keys.

What are you doing?

"Well, I'll need a target to aim at. Can you find a safe place for me to train?" Hal replied.

Ah, I see. I'll see if I can find a place. Make sure you get a bucket.

"For what?"

Water. In case something catches on fire.

"Good idea."

Hal then went to the hardware store and picked up her supplies. After she made the target, she set it and the bucket aside. She then put on the band and transformed into Shimmer.

"Where to, Roman?"

There's a lake South of you that has an abandoned dock.

She grabbed the target and bucket and took off. Roman directed her where to go until she got there. After a few minutes of flying, she got there and landed at the abandoned dock. She set her target and the bucket down before looking around. The lake was nice and there were hardly any people there, which was a big plus. The lake's shore was covered in small rocks, which meant she had to be careful with how she stepped. She then set up her target on dry land, a few steps away from the lake's edge. She kept the bucket by her just in case.

So, try blasting your target with your hand blasts.

She aimed her palm at her target and blasted. It threw her back and she hit the bush behind it, causing it to set fire. She felt her face heat up and she quickly filled the bucket with water. She then poured the water over the fire until it was put out. She felt so embarrassed, but Hal wasn't one to give up so easily, especially on this. So, she planted her feet and tried again, multiple times. Then, she finally hit the target with ease. Roman then taught her more spells as she progressed. He taught her how to shoot lightning, double hand beams, energy balls and how to alternate with ease. She wasn't the best, but they knew with more training she'd be great.

Before they could go over the spells again, Roman got an alert for downtown. There was a strange being attacking people. He told Hal and she was on it. She hid the bucket and target below the dock and underneath some tarp that had been left behind. She took off and flew through the cool Arizona air and made her way to the scene of the attack. She landed on her feet a few feet from the being that was attacking. It was a large, muscular humanoid being, and covered in black hair. The black hair covered its entire body, even the face. It almost looked like an ape, but it wasn't an ape. Whatever it was, it was destroying public property and putting people in danger. Hal's brows furrowed at the sight before her. She had never seen anything like this before.

"Hey!" Hal shouted. Once it looked at her, she froze. "Roman, what now?"

Blast it! He responded quickly.

She nodded and blasted its shoulder. That didn't do much of anything, except make it angry. As it made its way closer to her, she blasted it again but with lightning. The lightning stopped it in its tracks and caused its feet to push into the ground as it made its way closer to her. Hal used all of her strength to keep it at bay. Until suddenly, it grabbed her by the collar and punched her in the face. It was *far* stronger than her. Hal managed to blast it with an energy beam to get it off of her. The being rushed at her once it got its footing, but she stopped its fists in their tracks. Lightning surrounded her arms as she pushed harder. Then, the lightning shocked the being, taking it down to the ground. She marched over to it and grabbed it by the arm before taking off.

She took it to a rooftop and set the being down. The being sat against a wall as she crouched next to it.

"Who are you?" She questioned.

"Seek... seeking..." The being groaned out. Lightning surrounded her one arm.

"Tell me who you are," she demanded as the electricity flowed through her and around her arm.

Shock him. Roman said. Hal could hear the coldness in his voice, it was terrifying. She set a finger on its arm causing a shock through the monster's body.

"I work for Esimed," the being groaned out to get her to stop.

Ask him where he is, Roman said.

"Where is he?" She asked, now placing her full hand on its arm ready to shock it again.

"I only seek for the stone, I am a Seeker," it told her. She shocked him again. It groaned, "I will never tell you."

Then, the being died. Hal's eyes widened and she stepped back. She couldn't have killed it. The lightning around her arm disappeared and so did the being. She quickly collected herself and went back to the scene. A small crowd started to gather around her. She forced a smile and nodded to them.

"What was that... thing?" One woman asked.

"A Seeker, he's here as a worker for a much larger threat but don't worry, I'm taking care of it. I'll keep you all safe," Shimmer responded. With that, she took off.

She landed in her backyard and took off the band. She made her way to the kitchen and did some first aid to her face before heading to her room. She was still in disbelief of what had just transpired. She killed something, a living breathing being. She didn't know if she could live with herself. If being Shimmer meant that she had to be a killer, she didn't want to do it. Luckily, Roman didn't pick up on her emotional cues and continued going on about how he would find out more about the Seeker.

"That's great, Roman," Hal responded, "I'm going to bed."

Oh. Alright. I'll continue looking into this. Goodnight.

-

5 |

The next day, Hal's little speech about the Seeker was viral. People started questioning her as a hero and if she would actually be able to protect them. The whole battle between her and the Seeker was also caught on camera. So, she kept watching it over and over again to see what she could improve on. She let out a groan as she adjusted the ice pack on her eye. The painkillers she took were helping but the ice stung against her skin. She had to ask Roman if there was a healing spell because she didn't know what to say to her friends. She shifted in her seat at her desk, if only she took the day off. Instead, she was taking an extended break. She had to figure out what was going on or hope that Roman had figured it out. She was scared of the fact that she killed that Seeker and Roman didn't stop her. She shuddered at the thought.

"Haley," her manager pulled her away from her watching the video, "why are you on your phone?"

"I, uh," Hal started.

"If I catch you on your phone one more time, I'm gonna write you up," her manager told her.

She nodded and put her phone away. Then, she started doing her job, answering the phone. She couldn't stop thinking about the Seeker though. Roman still hadn't got back to her and there wasn't much she could do. Finally, lunch came around. She met up with her friends, hoping that they didn't doubt Shimmer.

"Hey, Hal!" Nicole greeted. She was finally back at work, which was very nice. Nicole being back at work meant things were going back to almost normal.

"Hey," Hal smiled. She sat down next to Nicole and across from Chris. He noticed the bruise on her eye and was instantly worried.

"Hal, what happened to your eye?" Chris asked, worry evident in his voice. Hal felt a wave of panic rush over her.

Say you got into a fight.

They all looked at Hal, waiting for a response as she just stared at Chris. She didn't know what to say and she knew Roman's excuse wouldn't work.

"Uh, Hal? Is everything okay?" He asked, more worried.

"I-" Hal started, "I'd rather not say, it's very embarrassing."

"I'm sure it's not that bad," Ariana said.

"You can tell us," Nicole said gently. Hal looked between them, thinking of a really good reason.

"Okay," Hal replied, "I was pulling up my sheets and it turns out, I tucked them too tight."

Nicole furrowed her brows, "Oh, okay."

"That sucks," Chris replied, "I hope you feel better soon, though."

"Yeah, me too," Ariana said.

"Thanks, you guys," Hal smiled.

You need a better excuse.

Then, they talked about the weekend ahead and the calls they had. Hal was zoned out into her world about the Seeker. She needed to set a boundary with Roman since she didn't want to kill again. She only tuned in when they started talking about Shimmer.

"So, that little speech that Shimmer gave," Chris started, "do you think more of those Seekers will show up? I don't doubt that Shimmer will take them down. I just hope that was the last of them."

"Yeah, that thing was terrifying to look at. I wonder how Shimmer is dealing after seeing something like that," Ariana replied and shook off that thought, "I hope that was the last of them, too."

"Yeah, me too. What if one showed up here? I don't think security would let Shimmer in to save us," Nicole joked.

They all laughed. Hal let out a chuckle, but then thought more about that. She figured that everyone would let her in to save people from Seekers or bad guys in general. But this was also her work, she thought that maybe they wouldn't let Shimmer in. Before she could spiral down that hole, the TV volume turned up.

"This just in, a robbery is in progress at a bank downtown." The reporter stopped and listened to her earpiece, "I've just gotten word that it is now a hostage situation. Shimmer, if you're hearing this, please help."

Hal stood, "I have to go."

Hal rushed out of there and found a place she could safely put on the band and transform. Once she was Shimmer, she was off to go save the day. When she landed, she found the cop in charge and talked to her. The officer was grateful she showed up and asked if Shimmer could head in and take care of the situation. Shimmer nodded and took off to fly around the bank to the back entrance. She quietly made her way to the lobby where the hostage situation was taking place. She snuck up behind the robber who unfortunately heard her. He spun around and shot at her. The bullet fell to the floor only causing it to sting against her skin.

"Shimmer, didn't plan you showing up," the robber stated.

"You should always plan for me," Shimmer responded. She then marched forward and landed a punch on him. She then restrained him the same way she did at the shooting, with her magic rope she created. She dragged the robber out to the cops who promptly arrested him after he was in cuffs, she went back to help the hostages out.

After they were all outside, a chubby little girl came up to her and tugged on her cape. Shimmer got down on a knee to the little girl's level.

"Are you okay?" She asked the little girl. The little girl nodded.

"I was wondering if my mommy can take a picture of us?" The little girl asked. Shimmer beamed.

"Of course," Shimmer replied. The mother came over and the two posed as the picture was taken. The mother thanked Shimmer before they headed out. A couple more people came over to thank her. Hal made herself a promise right then and there. To always try to stay after the enemy, whether it be a human or creature, and check on the victims. After people stopped coming up to her the head officer came up and thanked her as well. She then flew off and headed back to her work, hoping she wasn't late.

So, she was late. Lunch had ended and her friends messaged her, making sure she was okay. She responded to them saying that yes, she was fine. Hal pulled out her earbuds and started a livestream of the local news to see if they were talking about her and they were. She listened to them as she worked. She loved hearing them comment and talk about Shimmer. It was still cool to her. She figured she would never get over hearing people talk about her. It warmed her heart and brought the biggest grin to her face.

Suddenly, she got an email from her boss to meet her at her desk right away. Hal felt a pit in her stomach and tightness form in her chest. She quickly finished up the call she was on and then headed over to her boss' desk and knew what was coming. She was on her phone and late returning from lunch. She feared the worst.

However, the meeting wasn't as bad as she thought. Her manager gave her a stern warning and told her that she had two more strikes before a write-up of being late. Hal breathed a sigh of relief when she made it back to her desk. It really could've been a lot worse.

At the end of the day, Nicole met up with Hal so they could go home. Thankfully, they were working the same shift and decided to eat out that night. They decided on a local diner. It was one of their favorite places to go. At dinner they talked about their day.

"So, at lunch, when you left, was everything okay?" Nicole asked before taking a bite of food.

"Yeah, I just needed time away," Hal replied. Nicole didn't believe her but accepted it.

"You know, Chris was very worried about you," Nicole said with a grin. Hal felt her face heat up.

"He, he was?" She asked, trying to sound nonchalant.

"Yep. When are you gonna ask him out?"

"I don't know, I was kinda hoping he would."

"You know, you can't just hope for it to happen, sometimes life needs a push."

"Yeah, but-"

"The worst he can say is no. Just go for it."

"I'll try," Hal said with a sigh.

"Hey," Nicole started gesturing to her own eye, "what *really* happened to your eye?"

"I was pulling up my sheet and I hit myself," Hal quickly covered.

"Uh-huh," Nicole nodded.

The rest of dinner was fun and filled with laughter. When they got home, Nicole stayed up to watch tv at a low volume and Hal went to bed. Being Shimmer was really exhausting. Sure, she did get punched in the face and attacked and all that, but she loved being a superhero. This was her dream come true.

After Hal changed, she laid in bed and stared at the ceiling. So much had happened the last few days and it was all starting to hit her. She went to wipe away the tears as they started to fall from her eyes but remembered her black eye.

"Roman?" Hal whispered.

Yes?

"Is there a healing spell or something?" She asked.

Unfortunately, there isn't. We're going to have to find better excuses for you.

"Oh, okay," she said. She let out a sigh and closed her eyes. Her thoughts started to fade as she fell asleep.

-

I don't think this is the best way to find Esimed. Roman stated.

"Of course, it is," Hal replied. She was standing on the rooftop of a tall building downtown and overlooking the city.

We can't just wait for something to happen.

"We can and we will. Besides, what if someone needs Shimmer?" Hal asked. She was already transformed into Shimmer. She had nothing to do on Saturday, so, here she was on patrol.

I really doubt that.

"Crime never takes a break, Roman." Hal said while trying to hold back a smile, she knew that she sounded cheesy.

As if on cue, sirens blared in the distance. Hal ran over to the other side of the building to see the firetruck and ambulance fly by. Hal smiled and she heard Roman groan. He told her where the sirens were heading. They were heading to a robbery happening at a gas station three blocks over. She took a few steps back and then ran towards the edge of the building. She jumped off and then flew in the direction she needed to go. Adrenaline started to pump through her veins. She made it there before any authorities could show up.

"Hand over the money!" One of the robbers shouted at the poor cashier. Hal snuck in behind them. The cashier saw her and lit up, causing the robbers to spin around.

Shimmer set her hands on her hips, "What's up, guys?"

"Shimmer?" The one that was yelling at the cashier said.

"Yeah, that's me," Shimmer took a small step towards them, "If you wouldn't mind handing the money back over and turning yourselves in, it'd be greatly appreciated."

The other one threw a punch and Shimmer dodged it. Then, burglar one, he spoke, "How about we just take the money and run?"

"That's not gonna work," She replied. Burglar two then shot at her but the bullets fell to the ground, to their surprise. She raised a brow at them, "Neither is that."

Then, they threw punches at each other. Shimmer managed to give each one a black eye. Luckily, they didn't land any on her. She then heard the sirens outside and police talking over the megaphone. She smirked, she got her magic rope and tied them up. She grabbed their money bag and handed it back to the cashier.

"Here you are," she said.

The cashier smiled, "Thank you, Shimmer."

"Not a problem, ma'am," she responded. Shimmer then turned and walked out the door, "I have the burglars tied up!"

"Alright," an officer came up to her, "thank you."

"Of course, officer," Shimmer responded with a curt nod. There were a few people gathered around and they were given the go-ahead to say hi to Shimmer. Hal stayed and greeted everyone. Once everyone was satisfied and the cops had their bad guys, she took off back to the building she was at previously.

Hours passed and nothing else was happening. Hal let out a sigh, she was getting bored. She had been floating parallel to the ground, still atop the building. Roman was researching Esimed, seeing if he could find out when he would strike next or find his magical signature.

"What's a magical signature?" Hal asked as she placed her hands on her stomach.

A magical signature is a type of energy that everyone and everything has. The more involved with magic and or the dark arts that thing or person is, the higher the signature. Roman explained to her.

"So, you can find Esimed with it?" Hal tilted her head. She figured that it would be easier now.
In theory, yes. He replied. He kept tapping away at the screens in his ship but was unsuccessful in finding anything for Esimed.

"Any luck?" Hal asked after a beat of silence.

No. He must've cast a spell to hide himself. Maybe he knows I'm here. Hal, you could be in serious danger if he knows I'm the one that gave you the band. Hal could hear the worry in his voice.

"I'm sure I'll be fine, Roman. I promise not to tell him how I got the band," she responded with a small smile on her face.

I trust you.

"And I trust you." Suddenly, Hal remembered something. "Crap," Hal said and landed on her feet. "I was supposed to meet up with my friends at Brisco."

I thought that wasn't until six. Roman said. Hal flew down to where she parked her car and took off the band. She then checked the time.

"Yeah, that's in an hour and it's gonna take me that long to get there," she replied frantically. "How am I gonna keep this band with me, it can't stay in my purse."

Put it on your wrist, it'll adjust to you. Roman offered. She quickly put the band on her wrist and it turned into a bracelet. She then started her car and made her way to Brisco. She only arrived ten minutes late.

"Hal!" Ariana called her over. Hal met up with her friends by the entrance.

"Sorry, I'm late. Traffic," Hal said. They all nodded solemnly in agreement.

They headed in and got a lane so they could bowl. Brisco was basically an adult arcade. It did have kid friendly activities, but adults mostly flocked there. Brisco also had other activities such as VR Gaming, an arcade, billiards, laser tag, mini golf, and more. As they were getting set up the sound of pins hitting the wood lanes resonated in Hal's ears. It was a satisfying sound to her. Then, she heard the music that collided with the pins falling down, laughter, and talking. It was loud but not too loud. She recognized the song that was on and moved her shoulders a little bit to the music. She quickly stopped when Nicole got her attention.

They went over to their lane and started putting on their shoes. Ariana had gotten hers on at lightning speed and was already getting drinks for everyone. Hal sat in between Nicole and Chris as they got everything set up. Jeff was setting up the names in the machine. As they were putting on their shoes, Nicole nudged Hal and gave her an expectant look. Hal shook her head and went back to putting on her shoes. Nicole rolled her eyes.

"Hey, Chris," Nicole started, "Hal has something to ask you."

Hal turned her head to Nicole and mouthed 'No-no-no.' Nicole smiled and winked before leaving out of eyesight. Hal looked back at Chris. He was gorgeous. He always listened to her intently, even if it was just about a new movie. He'd stand up for anyone being mistreated even if it got him trouble at work. He always had a knack for making her smile even when she felt at her lowest. She loved that about him, how he always looked at the positive side of things. He was a good person and someone that Hal had fallen hard for. Hal was currently gazing into his beautiful eyes.

"What's up, Hal?" Chris said, bringing her back down to earth.

"Uhm," Hal blinked a few times, "how was, how was your day?"

Nicole slapped her forehead and went off to go help Ariana. Chris let out a chuckle. He thought she was adorable. Hal mentally slapped herself for not just going for it and asking him out.

"My day was good, how was yours?" He replied with an amazing smile. It made Hal feel weak in the knees. Luckily, she was sitting.

"It was... boring," Hal replied carefully. She wanted to say that she was out patrolling the streets waiting for Esimed to show up and that she stopped a burglary. However, that's not something she *should* say.

"I'm sure it's not gonna be boring anymore, now that we're here," he told her. Hal let out a small laugh. They shared a smile together. Unknown to both of them, they had moved and shifted closer together. She kept glancing at his lips and admired how kissable they looked. Chris was about to say something when Jeff came over.

"Alright," Jeff said, "all ready. Where's Ariana and Nicole?"

"They went to get drinks," Hal said. She was a little annoyed that Jeff came over but there wasn't much she could do about it. Chris was still gazing at her. He always admired how confident she was. He loved looking into her kind eyes and he loved how gentle she was with tough situations, like losing someone. He had fallen for and he hoped to gain enough confidence to ask her out one day.

Jeff huffed out a sigh with a roll of his eyes. He was about to make a comment when Ariana and Nicole came over. Once everyone was ready, it was time to start bowling. Jeff was up first as per usual. He always bragged about how good he was at bowling, but he always threw spares. He threw one-nine spares and an occasional gutter ball. He went up to the lane and threw the first ball. It was a gutter ball to Jeff's disappointment. Then, he threw his second ball. Hal tilted her head to the side as she watched the ball. It then moved to the gutter. Jeff huffed out a sigh and spun around.

"Damn it," Jeff cursed, "I really thought that was going to be a strike."

"Only in your dreams, Jeff," Ariana commented. She took a swig of her drink, "My turn!"

Ariana got up and grabbed her ball before she rolled it down the lane. They all watched her ball roll down the lane and then knock down all the pins. Ariana spun around with a huge grin on her face. The girls shared high fives and congrats.

"Did you guys see Shimmer's latest save?" Chris asked as Ariana went up for the second part of her turn.

"Yeah!" Nicole replied as she set her drink back down, "It was cool!"

"I bet she's getting paid by the place so they can get business," Jeff stated. Hal rolled her eyes.

"She could be doing it because, I don't know, the kindness in her heart?" Hal offered. Her lips pressed into a line. She was getting upset. Jeff always managed to get under her skin in some way and she hated that.

"No one's that nice," Jeff responded. Ariana came back over. Hal felt her jaw clench, she was over Jeff's rude comments. Then, it was Nicole's turn to go bowl.

"What are we talking about?" Ariana asked.

"Shimmer's latest save," Chris responded. Ariana mouthed an 'oh.' Chris continued, "I think she is. Shimmer *can* be a decent human being."

"Whatever, it's cause you're into *that* type of girl," Jeff responded and rolled his eyes.

"Anyway," Chris said, changing the subject, not wanting to listen to Jeff anymore, "wasn't Tyler supposed to meet us here?"

"He was but he couldn't make it." Jeff said. He was upset that Tyler couldn't make it, but he still tagged along because he wanted to see Nicole.

"That's unfortunate," Ariana said with the slightest hint of sarcasm.

A beat of silence fell over the group. Then, it was Hal's turn. She went up and threw the ball before watching it roll down the lane. She spun around once all of the pins fell, "Yes!"

"Hell yeah, girl!" Nicole high fived Hal. She then did her second turn and got herself another strike. Jeff muttered something about this was rigged under his breath and then went up to bowl. Hal then decided to get them a pizza.

Out of nowhere the ground began to shake and there was an explosion outside. Hal met up with her friends and they went outside to see what was going on. That's when they saw him, a man dressed in red and black. He wore a black cape, a grey-almost black sleeveless tunic, underneath that was a deep red, long sleeve shirt and pants. He wore gold bracers, gold shin guards, and a gold waist band that covered up most of his torso. He was tall and had black hair. His hair was pulled back and went down to his shoulders. Orange-red energy surrounded him. Seekers appeared from the parking lot, destroying the place.

Hal, that's him. That's Esimed. Roman said to her.

"Shit," Hal said under her breath.

"Who is that?" Nicole asked.

"I don't know," Ariana replied. Suddenly Esimed shot an energy beam a few feet away from them. They all jumped out of the way and landed hard on the ground. Chris made sure to protect Hal as they landed out of the way. He then helped her up and she brushed herself off.

"I, uh, thank you," she said, flustered.

"Are you okay?" He asked her as he looked her over.

"Yeah, I'm fine," she replied. Chris then turned to check on everyone else. As soon as no one was looking at her, Hal ran off to transform into Shimmer. She found her way into the bathroom and removed the band from her wrist. She was shaking. Hal took a deep breath before putting on the band. The familiar blue-white energy surrounded her, turning her into Shimmer. She ran out and flew into the air to float across from Esimed.

"Who are you?" Hal demanded. She had to internalize the fear that racked through her body. She couldn't let Esimed know that she was terrified. Hal put her fists on her hips subconsciously.

Esimed laughed, "You must be Shimmer." His voice was thick and threatening, "I've heard that you'll take me down? Well come on, take me down."

"Answer my question." Hal kept her fists at her sides, already feeling energy and magic running through her veins.

"Alright," he then made his voice loud enough for the citizens to hear, "My name is Esimed, and I am here for the Sunset Stone. It is my *mission* to find it. I will find it at *any* cost," he then looked directly at Hal, voice at a normal volume, "did that answer your question?"

"Yeah. It did," she responded monotonously. Hal could then feel the energy forming around her arms as she grew anxious. She may have had a brave, and annoyed, face on but she was freaking out on the inside. She could feel how threatening he was just by his own energy radiating from him.

"Well, go on. Come at me," he threatened with his arms open. He fully expected her to start throwing punches. He could tell that she was new to this, he could see it in her eyes.

To his surprise, Hal took a deep breath and shot an energy beam at him. He stopped it mid-air and threw it back at her. It threw her to the roof of Brisco, causing her to slide on her back and to a stop. She proceeded to prop herself up on her elbows. Esimed floated over to her. Hal forced herself to stand. She flew back up at him and was able to land an uppercut punch on him. He was thrown back a bit. He straightened himself out and rubbed his jaw, shocked at her strength.

"Nicole!" Hal heard Ariana's voice and her head snapped in that direction. Nicole was lying unconscious on the ground. Hal started to fly over but Esimed grabbed her with his own magic rope around her throat. Hal's hands immediately went to the rope to try and break free.

He leaned to her ear, his voice menacing "You're coming with me."

"He's got Shimmer!" Someone shouted. A portal appeared behind them, and they disappeared along with all the Seekers.

Out of nowhere, Hal was pulled down by her wrists and onto her knees. She saw that she was chained and shackled. However, these chains and shackles had inscriptions and an orange energy glowing around them. She then looked around to see where she was. He had brought her to a small arena of sorts. There was large, what used to be, windows and piles of red and yellow plastic rectangles under them. Hal didn't recognize where she was, and it terrified her.

"Shimmer," Esimed started, and he pointed to his forehead as he talked, "how did you get that band?"

"I'm not telling you," she refused. She couldn't break her promise to Roman. He dropped his hand and closed his fists. She looked at the ground of fear while trying to suppress tears that threatened to spill.

He used magic to make her look at him directly in the eyes then spoke, "It's imperative that you tell me, *now*."

"No," she forced out. He rolled his eyes and let go of her. Her head jerked away at the release. She then kept her eyes trained on him.

He shocked her with a lightning bolt. She yelped out in pain and fell to her side. Even if it hurt her, she couldn't tell him where she got the band. That could give away who she was and put Roman in more danger. She kept her mouth shut as best she could. He used his magic to make her sit up between shocks, he wasn't going to let her off easy. He kept shocking her with lightning and by the fourth time she broke. Her eyes were on the ground now as she recovered from the constant lightning strikes.

"Fine," she choked out, "it was delivered to me. I don't know who sent it."

"You don't know *who* sent it to you?" He asked. Orange-red lightning surrounded his hand, ready to strike.

Hal huffed out a sigh and looked at him, "Yeah, what else would that mean?"

"Dammit," he cursed under his breath. The cackling of the lightning filled the silence filling the room.

"Are you going to kill me?" Hal asked, breaking the growing silence, "Or are you going to tell me your plan?"

"I'm not going to kill you, you're not strong enough to take me down and that would be unfair. I like a fair fight," he replied bluntly. Hal had a look of offence cross her face. He rolled his eyes, "Don't act so offended, you know it too."

Hal put on her brave face, "So, you're going to tell me your master plan?"

"No," he looked at her with his brows furrowed, "that would be idiotic."

"It wouldn't be for you," Hal mentioned with a small tilt of her head. He just kept staring at her with his eyes slightly squinted. She looked more familiar to him now that he was seeing her in person. Suddenly, it hit him, and he knew who she was. The band on her forehead, the costume, her powers, all meant she could be who he thought she was to the timeline.

"Parker," he said. Hal's eyes widened. He smirked, "That name mean something to you?"

"Nuh-no, it doesn't," she responded, trying to conceal her fear. She swallowed; fear was trying to claw its way to take over her. She had to get out of there and away from him as fast as possible.

"It should since it's your last name," He towered over her, "I'm the one who ended your great granddaughter's life. She looked so much like you; it was a shame she had to die."

"You *what*?" Hal's fear turned to frustration.

"Oh? No one told you? Not even her best friend?" He questioned. Hal looked away not wanting to believe what he was saying. Esimed continued, "Ah, what was the best friend's name? Oh yes, that's right, *Roman*. Is he here? He's the one who gave you that band, isn't he?"

Hal's head shot up at him. He smirked; he now knew who she was to the timeline. Suddenly, there was blue-white lightning wrapped around her arms. Her eyes turned blue-white with little lightning bolts coming out. He took a step back. He had never seen this before, not even the original wearer did that. She broke free of the chains and shackles, then charged at him. She held him by the collar as she dragged him against the desert floor then she took him to the sky. In fear, he created another portal before disappearing again. All the energy and lightning faded away as her eyes returned to normal. She hovered in the air, reeling from this information.

"Roman?" Her voice cracked. "Roman, can you hear me?"

Yes, I can hear you. I'm so sorry, I've been trying to get to you but there was a barrier and-

"Did he kill my great granddaughter?" She felt her eyes starting to well up.

Yes. She fought to the end.

"And you were her best friend?"

How-? Yes, I was. I should've told you.

"I don't want to talk to you for a bit. I need to process this. But before I do, can you help me find a way to Nicole? I have to see her," Hal told him. She knew if she reacted right then and there she could ruin all of this, so she kept her mouth shut. She would process her emotions and come back in a much better state of mind.

Of course. Roman said. He was upset with himself; he knew that he should've told her sooner.

Roman gave her directions to the hospital that Nicole was at. Hal landed at the entrance to the hospital and secretly transformed back into herself and put the band back on her wrist. She pulled out her phone from her back pocket and saw she had several texts and voicemails from Ariana. The last text was Nicole's room number and something along the lines of if she was going to show up at all. Hal mentally prepared herself for the worst. She knew she was going to get an earful based on the texts and voicemails. Finally, Hal made it to Nicole's room. Ariana saw her and was immediately in the hallway with her.

"Where have you been?" Ariana asked, anger in her voice, "I have been trying to reach you and nothing?! What the fuck, Hal?"

"I'm so sorry, I just- I was-" Hal stopped herself and shook her head, "I have no excuse. Please let me see her."

"No, you ran off at the first sign of danger and then didn't even come back when she was unconscious-"

"She was unconscious?" Hal asked. Her worry was starting to bubble into tears.

"Save it, Hal-"

"Hal?" Nicole's voice pulled them away from their argument, "Is she there? Can I see her?"

Ariana let out a huff and walked away. Hal wiped away her tears and walked into the hospital room to see her best friend. It killed Hal to see Nicole like this. She had gone through too much. Hal blamed herself for this one. Esimed probably tracked her the same way they were tracking him.

"Hal, come sit," Nicole gestured to the chair next to the bed. Hal went over and sat in it. She took Nicole's hand in hers. Nicole had a small smile on her face.

"Nini, I'm so, *so sorry*. I should've taken you with me and-"

"Hey, you know that this isn't your fault, right?" Nicole said. Hal gave a tight smile. If only she could tell her. Hal knew this was all her fault.

"I guess you're right," Hal responded. She was holding back tears and could feel the painful prickling in her nose that told her to cry.

"Of course, I am. I heard Shimmer was taken by the guy that attacked. I wonder where she is," Nicole looked down at her lap, "I hope she's safe now."

"Me too," Hal said distantly. She brought herself back, "So, when do you get to come home?"

Nicole let out a small laugh, "Hopefully tomorrow."

"Thank God, the house would be so boring without you. I don't know how I'll survive tonight," Hal joked. Nicole let out another small laugh. Hal glanced at the clock and figured visiting hours would be ending soon. Hal patted Nicole's hand, "I'm gonna go get the house ready for you. I'll see you tomorrow, okay?"

"I want it perfect, flowers and everything," Nicole joked. Hal leaned over and hugged her. Nicole rubbed her back, "this isn't your fault, Hal. It never will be."

Hal pulled away and gave her a nod with a smile. Then, Hal got an idea. She exited the hospital and found a safe spot to transform into Shimmer. She then flew up to Nicole's room and landed as she entered Nicole's room. Nicole sat up at the sight.

"Shimmer?" Nicole whispered.

"That's me," she then walked closer and stood at Nicole's bedside.

"How did you find me?" Nicole asked.

Shimmer set her hands on her hips and shrugged, "Well, after every event I make it a point to speak with *all* the victims. I heard you were hurt pretty bad. So, I wanted to come see if you were alright."

"I'm alright, thanks," Nicole said.

"Good, I'm glad," Shimmer went to step back out through the window.

"Shimmer?" Nicole had a sense of hesitance in her voice.

"Yes?" Shimmer said as she looked back at Nicole.

"I just- I just wanted to say thank you. I was at that concert and without you, I wouldn't have been able to see my best friend again. And I just- thank you." Nicole was wiping away some tears. Shimmer got her a tissue from the counter in the room.

"You're welcome. I will always be there to save you," Shimmer said. She started to turn around to take off, but Nicole stopped her.

"What happened today? I heard you disappeared, are you alright?" Nicole asked, concern evident in her voice.

Shimmer spun around, "I'm fine, just a run in with a bad guy. I'm taking care of it, no need to worry."

"I know you'll take care of it." Nicole gave her a smile and Shimmer smiled back. They waved to each other before Shimmer took off into the night.

-

Esimed was wide eyed as he stood in the construction site that he hid out in. He had never seen Eliana, his former foe, that powerful. He didn't even know if she had been capable of it. He was terrified for a moment; his opponent was far more powerful than he knew. He didn't know if she knew how powerful she was yet. He took a breath and calmed down. He focused on what he knew and that was that Shimmer was new and didn't know anything yet. He still had the upper hand even if Roman was helping her.

He was more powerful and more experienced than Shimmer, he knew he could win. Then, he planned to take them both out. If he killed Shimmer and Roman, he wouldn't have to face them again. He figured to do this after the ritual with the sunset stone so it would be easier to accomplish his mission.

-

It had been three days since Hal was captured. She was ready to talk it out with Roman which would have to wait until after work. She was still formulating what to say. She kept getting long calls throughout the day, so she had some time to work out what she was going to say. She upgraded to a police scanner app and had that going on in the background. It was a slow day up until the scanner was reporting on the Seekers showing up at one of the casinos. Hal ended her call quickly, transformed, and was off to the casino.

There were only a few Seekers there. Hal punched one in the face instantly regretting it because it didn't do much of anything. She shook her hand and then hit it with an energy ball. It took a couple more tries and some lightning, but she finally knocked it out. Then, the next two, she hit them with lightning. Each of them took three hits to knock them out. She then talked to the victims and listened to them thank her before she left for work. She had arrived back just in time for lunch. She met up with her friends and they talked about the usual. Hal was really getting the hang of this being a superhero business. Or at least she felt that she was.

By the way, there's a large magic signature at the Grand Canyon. It could be worth investigating, Roman said very cautiously.

"So," Hal started, "since it's been so stressful, I was thinking we could all take a road trip to the Grand Canyon?"

"Hal," Nicole started, "it's a big hole in the ground, why?"

"It's in state and close?" Hal offered with a brow raised.

"That sounds like fun, can the guys tag along?" Chris asked. Hal glanced at Nicole, looking for approval. Nicole gave her a curt nod.

"Yeah, if you want to join us," Hal replied. She looked at Ariana.

"Sounds like fun, I'm in," Ariana said. Hal smiled.

"Awesome, leave Friday and come back Sunday night?" Hal asked.

"Sounds like a plan," Nicole smiled at Hal.

They continued finalizing plans and getting hotel rooms. Hal then excused herself. She figured now was a good chance to reconcile with Roman. She found a secluded spot where no one would give her weird looks for talking to herself.

"Roman?" She asked.

Yes?

"Look, I kinda get why you hid the details from me," she started, "I'm still not happy about it. I wish you would've told me sooner, but I forgive you. It's a hard topic for you and I know you'd tell me eventually. It just sucked hearing it from our enemy."

I- Haley. I'm so sorry he told you. I should have told you sooner. From now on, I'll answer all your questions and tell you everything. I promise.

Hal smiled, "Thank you."

Eventually, lunch was over, and it was back to work. Unfortunately, Hal's bosses called her into the department office. Hal sat in the chair across from the desk, her manger next to her and her department head across from her. Her leg was bouncing. She cursed herself for not taking an anti-panic attack pill before this meeting.

"So, Haley," the department head, Jason, started, "we noticed that you've been logging off a lot. What's going on?"

"Uhm," Hal said, "life."

"Haley," Linda started, "that's not a good answer. If it's your panic attacks, that's okay but please try to stay at your desk more."

You cannot tell them. Roman warned her. Hal let out an internalized sigh, this was suddenly harder than she thought.

"It's my panic attacks. Maybe I need to see the counselor now?" Hal said.

"We can set that up, but you have to get this under control, Haley," Linda said.

"Let's go ahead and set up days for you to meet with the counselor, alright?" Jason offered.

Then, they came up with a plan to help Hal keep her job. While it was finalizing, there was a loud crash outside. Linda and Jason rushed out of the room and out of the building. Hal quickly went to a window to peek outside and see what was going on. There were Seekers in the parking lot. Hal had to quickly find a place that she could transform into Shimmer. She quickly made her way to the roof. Once she was on the roof, she quickly looked for the Seekers again. They were near the north-west entrance and there was a lot of them. They were turning over cars and causing a mess. Then, security showed up. One of the Seekers threw a car at the guard. Hal put the band on and then transformed. Then, she went and landed in front of the guard. She caused the car to bend slightly and stopped it from hitting the guard.

"Shimmer, thank you," the guard said. Shimmer spun around and helped the guard up.

"Of course, please keep the civilians safe, I'll take care of the Seekers," Shimmer said heroically. The guard nodded, rounding up the others to do what Shimmer said.

Shimmer was throwing punches, lightning balls, and energy beams at the Seekers. They were stronger than the last time and were not going down as easily. She cursed at the fact.

Maybe a lightning strike with an energy beam? Roman offered. Hal tried it and it worked. It knocked them back a peg.

"Hey, asshole!" A familiar voice yelled. Hal's head shot over to the source. It was Jeff. He was standing in front of one of the Seekers, taunting it. Hal heaved out a sigh. She hit the current Seeker before going over to take care of Jeff. Before she could, that Seeker with Jeff crushed him with a car. He was dead instantly. Hal stopped in her tracks.

"*Shit,*" Hal said under her breath.

She still quickly went over and started taking down the Seeker that killed Jeff. Once it was down, she lifted the car to check. He was dead. It was a gruesome sight and she wanted to throw up. Hal felt a pang of guilt. She could've been there sooner to save him, but she just had to be petty. She took those emotions and channeled them into taking down the last three Seekers. She spun around to see everyone staring in shock. Hal knew exactly why. Jeff died and it was her fault. Instead, the small crowd cheered, despite Jeff's death. She flew over and landed closer to them.

One guy ran up to her, "Thank you, Shimmer. For protecting us."

Hal shook his hand and gave him a smile. More came up and thanked her and took pictures. After she was sure everyone was done talking to her, she took off and landed on the other side of the building, out in the parking lot. She transformed back, putting the band on her wrist and slowly walked back over to her boss's office. Once she got there, they were gone. She huffed out a sigh and went back to her desk. There she had an email from both bosses stating that everything was finalized and all she had to do was sign. She glanced at the papers on her desk, noticing what they were. She grabbed a pen and signed. She kept telling herself what to do. She couldn't bear to think about what had just happened.

She logged back on to take calls. She still turned on her news stream, luckily nothing else had happened that day. Suddenly the news mentioned what had just happened and how there was only one casualty. Hal got off the phone and went to the little courtyard that was rarely ever visited. She sat on a bench underneath one of the trees. She put her phone in her pocket and took deep breaths. She tried so hard to convince herself that these things happened and that it wasn't her fault. She couldn't, though. She knew this was all her fault. Then, she let herself cry. She had all these emotions pent up since being captured by

Esimed and hadn't been able to talk about it with anyone. She then cried harder.

Anything I can do to help? Roman's voice was gentle. He was genuinely concerned about her. He wished he could see her in person and comfort her. Hal just shook her head. *Let me know if you do need something.*

Hal wiped away some tears when she heard the door open. She looked up and saw Chris. She didn't want him seeing her like this. He had a look of concern and sadness on his face. He walked over and took a seat next to her. He set an arm around her shoulders and gave her a hug.

"So, you heard?" Chris asked when letting go, still keeping an arm on her. His voice was laced with sadness. He was friends with Jeff, even if Jeff was kind of a dick.

Hal looked at him, "Yeah. It was so...terrifying."

"I know, I saw it all from inside. It's too bad Shimmer couldn't get to him," he said distantly. Hal shifted so that she was facing him more.

"Do you blame her?" She sniffled. She thought that maybe hearing someone else's thoughts would help her.

Chris looked into her eyes, "No. Shimmer is human as far as we know, and we all make mistakes. Sure, hers was on a larger scale but all in all, if Jeff would have let her handle the situation, he'd still be here." He ran a hand over his face, "Oh man, I shouldn't be talking about the recently deceased like that."

Hal got a small smile on her face, "People have said worse about actors that passed."

"Yeah," Chris said, now smiling too, "that's true."

"One more question," Hal said.

"What is it?" Chris felt butterflies in his stomach.

"Okay, well two," she said, "One, do you still trust Shimmer to protect us, and two are you still willing to go to the Grand Canyon this weekend?"

"I will always trust Shimmer, and yes. Tyler is still shaken up, but I got two other buddies that would be down, is that okay?" He replied.

"Sounds like a plan," she let go of a breath that she was holding.

She shifted herself back to look away. They sat in silence for a bit. Just listening to the sound of the wind moving through the leaves and the distant traffic from the highway nearby. Chris subconsciously pulled Hal closer and rubbed her shoulder. She then set her head on his shoulder. Chris felt a blush rise on his cheeks. He hoped that maybe over the weekend he could ask her out.

Hal suddenly sat up, "I need to get back to work."

"Yeah," Chris said, wishing she didn't remember, "I should too."

They stood up and hugged before saying goodbye. She went back to her desk and her boss was there.
"I'm so sorry," Hal started, "it's just, my sort of friend-"

"I know," Linda stopped her, "I saw everything. You and your friends have been dismissed for the rest of the week. I wanted to make sure you knew."

Hal was about to say something, but Linda walked away. Hal logged off and clocked out and then met Nicole at home.

Once Hal got home and set her stuff down, she looked for Nicole. She found her in her room, lying on the edge of the bed staring at the ceiling. Hal laid next to Nicole and turned her head and gazed at Nicole. Her brunette friend was lost in thought. She was lost in thoughts of worry, sadness, and anger.

"Nicole," Hal whispered. Nicole was now looking into Hal's eyes.

Nicole could see the tear stains on Hal's cheeks. Nicole reached over and brushed her hand over her friend's cheek. She returned her hand to her side before speaking, "Are you okay?"

"Yeah, I'm good. Are you okay?" Hal asked. Their voices were still quiet as if they were revealing secrets. Secrets that only they could know in the empty house.

"I'm alright. I'm still shaken up," Nicole glanced away then back at Hal, "I still want to go up north with you."

"How did-?"

"I know you, Hal."

"Oh, okay." They sat in silence for a beat. Hal then spoke, "Do you still trust Shimmer?"

Nicole's brows furrowed, "Of course. Why wouldn't I?"

"But don't you blame her for Jeff's death?" Hal could feel her throat closing up. She was ready to cry again. She swallowed down the emotion.

"No. If Jeff hadn't done what he did, he wouldn't have died. The sight was gruesome and something none of us should have seen and we should be shaken up by *that*," Nicole responded. She took a deep breath, "I will always trust Shimmer."

-

9

It was two days later and time to head north. Hal was more than excited. She was double checking that she had everything packed. Although she was going because of Shimmer reasons, she was still happy to go somewhere away from everything. She needed a distraction before she had a breakdown.

You've checked over your things five times now. Roman commented.

Hal shrugged, "I just like to make sure I have everything."

That's fair, but five times? Hal, you're being obsessive.

"Rude," Hal replied with a smile, "I just don't have a great memory and you keep distracting me!"

"Hal?" Nicole knocked at the door. Hal quickly grabbed her phone. Nicole opened the door, "Who are you talking to?"

"Chris, I'll text you? Okay bye," Hal pretended to hang up and gave a grin, "Was just talking to Chris."

"You had me worried, I thought you were going insane," Nicole jested. They shared a laugh.

"Nini, I'm already there, you knew this," Hal feigned being upset. The girls kept joking around. Roman listened to this all unfold from his ship, a smile formed on his face. He wished that he could go and talk to Hal face to face but it was too risky with Esimed out there.

"Are you packed? Ariana will be here soon," Nicole said.

Hal nodded, "Yeah. I checked five times."

"That's a little excessive," Nicole commented.

"No, it's not," Hal defended.

"Whatever you say. Let's get the car loaded up," Nicole replied then spun around and went to grab her own luggage. Once Nicole was definitely out of ear shot, Hal breathed a sigh of relief.

"Roman, how are we gonna take down Esimed? What if we run into him while we're there?" Hal questioned.

Fair questions. Well, for starters, you're not going to get captured this time.

"That's a good plan. Also, we have to find the sunset stone before Esimed does," Hal interjected.

Yes, I'll work on that. If we- you run into him, try to fight him. Use the magic rope to restrain him-

"What if that doesn't hold him?"

Good point. We could send him to another dimension, if you're okay with it.

Hal raised a brow, "Another dimension?"

Yes.

"Other dimensions exist?" Hal asked slowly as it started to hit her. Her brows furrowed and she was still in shock. She always figured that they existed but hearing it confirmed was a whole other deal. She sat at the edge of her bed and played with the band on her wrist.

Haley?

"Oh my God."

If time travel is possible, so is that.

"I know, it's just... Shocking, okay?" Hal replied. Her eyes widened, "Crap, Nicole is waiting on me."

The plan, though?

Hal slapped her forehead, "Yeah, that too. Okay, so, I get the Sunset Stone first and if he shows up, I stop him from getting it and send him into another dimension."

Okay, good plan. How are you gonna cast the spell?

"I'll figure that out when I get there," she responded quickly as she gathered her bags. She opened her door and took her stuff to the car. Hal looked at Nicole, who was standing at the trunk of her car, looking at her phone. Hal breathed a sigh of relief. She smiled, "Hey, sorry about that wait."

"It's fine," Nicole responded, "it wasn't that long, and Ariana is running late. The boys will be here soon. So, you're good."

"Oh, she is? Is she okay?" Hal asked as she packed her bags into the car. Both of them only had two bags, so they had plenty of room in Nicole's car for Ariana's stuff. Nicole looked up from her phone and to Hal.

"Not really, her boyfriend was being a jackass, to say the least. He showed up out of nowhere and well, they got into an argument. They broke up on the spot. Luckily, he left and she's safe," Nicole told her.

"And if he follows, we'll keep her safe," Hal responded as she shut the trunk. Nicole nodded in agreement. They were about to head back in when the boys pulled up. Chris waved at Hal, and she waved back.

Nicole leaned into Hal's ear, "Maybe you two could get some alone time?"

"Maybe," Hal responded. They quieted down when the three boys came up to them. Chris exchanged hugs with the girls, lingering with Hal a little longer.

"Where's Ariana?" Chris asked as he and Hal let go.

"She's running a little late, she should be here soon," Nicole responded.

"Oh," Chris said as he remembered, "let me introduce you guys," he gestured to his friends, "This is Brad," he gestured to the man who had blond hair, "and this is William," he gestured to the black-haired man. "Guys, this is Hal and Nicole."

"Nice to meet you," the girls said in unison as they shook hands. They then went inside and waited for Ariana to show up. It wasn't too long until Ariana showed up and the six were off.

Nicole drove ahead of the boys in the car while Chris followed shortly behind in his SUV. Ariana was in the back seat and Hal was in the passenger seat on her phone. She hoped that no one needed Shimmer while she was in the car. Nicole and Hal sang along to a song they loved that came on. During the song Ariana took a video of them singing along. Then, lunch rolled around. Luckily they had made it to Flagstaff, and they stopped for lunch there. They stopped at a local pizza place. It was the only thing that sounded appetizing.

Hal was uneasy the whole time. The lack of crime happening really affected her. It seemed like there wasn't even crime in Flagstaff. When they were at a rest stop, Roman assured her that he would let her know if there was any crime for her to stop. Hal's leg bounced as they all ate their pizza. Nicole set her hand on Hal's thigh, trying to calm her down.

"So, what else did you guys want to do while we were there?" Chris asked.

"We should definitely stock up on some booze while we're here. We could drink in the hotel room one night and hang out," Brad suggested.

"That could be fun," Ariana said before taking a bite of pizza.

Hal started feeling sick to her stomach. She set a hand over her stomach and tried to focus on the conversation. She couldn't, she felt tears threatening to spill. She excused herself and went outside. She breathed deeply and tried to calm down. She reached into her bag and pulled out her medicine. She quickly took one and waited. She waited some more and was still panicking. She closed her eyes and told herself that it was going to be okay.

"I can face him," she whispered it like a prayer, "I can face him. He knocked me down, but I got back up. I can face him. I got this."

She then noticed that her stomach wasn't hurting, and her heart rate had gone down. Her breathing was normal and there were no more tears. She felt calmer. She knew she could do this and face Esimed. Hal shook her hands out and went back inside.

"You okay?" Nicole whispered when Hal sat back down. Hal nodded.

"We should probably get going, don't want to be late for check-in," William suggested. The rest agreed. They paid for their food and picked up some booze from the local store. Then, in no time, were back on the road.

-

10

They had finally reached the Grand Canyon and were early for check-in at the hotel. So, they did some sightseeing. They parked by the hotel and all of them stretched as they got out of the cars. It was chilly outside, especially when there was a breeze. The smell of pine filled Hal's nose making her feel at ease. They were all standing on the rim trail that looked over the canyon itself. Hal was busy looking for a hole or a cave, somewhere in the canyon. Chris' hand on her shoulder spooked her and brought her back.

"Sorry, didn't mean to scare you," he said. His hand left her shoulder and he scratched the back of his neck.

"It's all good," she smiled. He smiled back and his hands fell at his sides. He felt so at ease with her. She then continued, "What's up?"

"Oh, we're gonna get a group photo over there," he gestured to the group behind him.

She nodded and they walked over to the group. They found someone to take the picture. The person taking the picture was about their age, so they knew how to take the picture. The person snapped a few on one phone. Instead of forcing this person to go through six phones, the one with the pictures sent it to everyone.

"This is such a cute picture," Ariana commented, "I'm definitely posting this one."

"Can you tag me?" Brad asked.

"Me too," William added.

Ariana laughed, "Of course."

Chris, Nicole, and Hal stepped away so they could talk.

"How are you holding up, Chris?" Nicole asked gently.

"I'm holding up, luckily, I have you guys," he responded with a small smile, but with his eyes focused on Hal.

"If you need anything, let us know," Hal mentioned. Chris pulled them into a group hug and thanked them.

It was then finally time to check into the hotel. The hotel was very rustic. The walls were dark almost black wood logs with animal heads on them. In each corner there was a sitting area. To the right of the entrance was a gift shop. Dead ahead was a red carpeted staircase. To the right of the staircase was the check-in desk. Hal took a deep breath. The place smelled like wood and fire. She could hear the cackling of the fire as she looked around and noticed all the animal heads. Since it felt like those animal heads were staring into her soul, Hal looked away and focused her attention in front of her. She then walked over to the check-in desk with Nicole. Hal set her hands on the tall desk, running her hands over the smooth dark wood.

The front desk woman greeted them and then checked them in. They had two rooms next to each other. The girls went into their room and the boys into theirs. Hal set her stuff down and sat on one of the beds. Ariana sat next to her.

"What do you think of Brad and William?" Ariana asked. Nicole sat on the other bed across from them.

"They seem nice," Nicole responded.

"Yeah, they do," Hal said. She felt her nerves build up. She couldn't stop thinking of the fact she could run into Esimed tonight. She feared that he would beat her again. She couldn't do that. She had to win this time.

"Hal?" Nicole asked, bringing her back to reality.

"What?" Hal replied. Nicole and Ariana shared a look.

"You've been acting weird today, are you okay?" Ariana asked with concern. Nicole bit her lip and she looked at Hal with all of the concern in the world. She didn't know what was going on with her friend and they told each other everything. It put a pit in Nicole's stomach.

"I'm good," Hal responded, "still shaken up after seeing Jeff end up like...that."

Nicole nodded, "It's okay, if you need something, let us know, okay?"

"I will," Hal said, "Are you guys okay?"

"Yeah, I'm good," Ariana replied.

"Me too," Nicole said.

Then, there was a knock at the door. Hal got up and went to answer it. She peeked through the peephole first. It was Chris and the boys. Hal opened the door with a smile.

"Hey," she greeted.

"Hey, we were wondering if you guys wanted to go get dinner?" Chris asked. Hal turned back and the girls were right behind her, they nodded. So, they went to dinner.

11

Later that night, they were all exhausted from driving so they decided to go to bed. Hal was grateful that they decided to sleep. She could look for the Sunset Stone while they were all sleeping. So, here she was waiting for her friends to sleep. The sun was well below the horizon and the full moon lit up the room.

They're asleep. Roman's voice came through.

"You sure?" Hal whispered. Roman had told her earlier that he could detect when they're sleeping very easily from his ship. Hal found it creepy, but she needed to be sure that they were asleep. After all, there were Shimmer things to do.

Yes. Time to go.

"Alright," Hal responded in a whisper. She carefully snuck out onto the balcony and transformed into Shimmer. Then, she was off. As she flew over to the canyon she spoke, "Roman, where am I heading?"

There's a cave that has a temple in it. Head east.

"Left or right?"

Seriously?

"Yes."

Right.

"Thank you."

Hal flew for a bit and started to wonder where this cave could be. She hoped it was coming up soon. She couldn't risk being out too long, her friends would get suspicious of her.

Okay you're coming up on it now. In three, two, now! Hal stopped. He continued, *To your left, there's a cave. It's the temple.*

Hal flew over to the cave and landed once she entered it. She looked around. It looked like any other cave. Until she walked deeper in. That's when it started looking like a temple. It was mostly made of gold with statues guarding an entrance. The walls and gold entrance were also covered in hieroglyphs that she didn't recognize. Hal went up close to one of the columns at the entrance and ran a hand over the hieroglyphs. Suddenly, they all glowed a yellow color and showered the cave in light. The entrance between the columns lit up a path to a pedestal. Hal carefully walked over to the pedestal and upon seeing it, there was a stone on it. The stone was literally the colors of the sunset. It was orange, purple, pink, and had some blue hues in it. It was gorgeous.

That's what he's after. The Sunset Stone.

"Care to elaborate?" Hal asked as she continued to admire the stone from a distance. She wasn't sure of what the stone could do and wanted to be careful.

From what I've read it's a stone that has the power to make you more powerful. It does need a ritual at a certain time of year to get said boost in powers.

"What happens when I just... touch it?" Hal had walked around the stone as she spoke. The stone seemed to be about the size of the palm of her hand.

It might put a surge of energy through you? I'm not quite sure.

Hal shrugged and picked it up. She expected something, anything to happen. Even for it to burn her, but nothing happened. Her brows furrowed, "Roman? Nothing's happening."

Okay that's weird, maybe I was wrong.

"What if I broke it?"

Did you actually break it?

"Probably, nothing's happening!" Hal shook it in her hand, hoping that would do something. Just as she was about to try something, the sound of gravel moving under feet grabbed her attention. She turned to face the noise. It was Esimed.

"You've no idea what you're dealing with," he threatened, "put the stone down."

"I know exactly what I'm dealing with," she replied confidently. He charged at her, and she dodged him. Then, she ran past him and flew out of the cave. She flew as fast as she could in the direction back to the hotel.

Suddenly a magic rope wrapped around her ankle, causing her to lose her balance. She was yanked back. While she was traveling back to Esimed, she turned herself over. Then, Esimed grabbed her by the collar and went right for the stone. In retaliation, Hal threw him a punch with her empty hand. She was able to land a punch on his nose causing him to let go of her and back away a foot or so. He shook his head while holding his nose. Hal was breathing heavily. She glanced down to see if the magic rope was gone. She saw that it was gone and went to fly away when Esimed threw more magic rope and made it wrap all the way around her. She kept the best grip she could on the stone.

He leaned in next to her ear and reached for the stone, "I'll be taking this."

She squeezed the stone in her hand but unfortunately, he was able to pry it from her grasp. As soon as he had it, he backed away from her with a smirk on his face. A portal formed behind him, and he disappeared. He was gone and so was the stone.

The magic rope around Hal disappeared and her hands flew to her face, and she started to cry. She felt defeated. She flew back to the hotel and landed on the balcony, out of sight. She took off the band, put it on her wrist, and was herself again. She walked into the room, seeing that her friends were asleep in the same bed, which Hal was grateful for. She went and flopped down on the other bed. She just wanted to hide away from the world. She failed the city. She wasn't able to stop Esimed and save everyone. She could feel herself start to cry again. How was she going to stop Esimed now?

12

The sun was up and so was Nicole and Ariana. Hal was still asleep, and Nicole went to go wake her up. Nicole found it strange that Hal was still asleep, usually Hal was up early. It was a habit she got from work. So, Hal should've been up by now. She must have been more tired than Nicole originally thought.

"Hal? It's time to get up," Nicole gently moved Hal's shoulder as she spoke.

"No," Hal groaned out. Nicole looked at Ariana and she shrugged.

"We're about to order some food," Nicole coaxed.

Hal groaned and sat up, "Okay, I'm up."

"Good," Nicole said.

The girls then went about and took their showers, one at a time. They had some music playing while they got ready, all singing along with a lot of enthusiasm. Hal tried her best to keep a happy face even though she just wanted to crawl back under the covers and hide away from everyone. She never thought that she would fail like this. She was the hero, wasn't she supposed to win against the bad guy?

She focused on enjoying getting ready with her friends. She had to keep her mind off of last night; if she didn't, she would sob all over again. She had finished applying her light makeup and waited for her friends. After they were all ready for the day, Hal received a text from Chris.

"Chris just texted me," Hal said, a smile forming on her face. Even though she still felt like crap from last night, her heart still fluttered at reading his name and text on her phone. She sat on the edge of the bed to read the text.

"Well?" Nicole said, "What did he say?"

"Yeah, what did he say?" Ariana said as she sat next to Hal.

Hal rolled her eyes, and she shook her head, "He just asked if we wanted to meet up for breakfast. Nothing special."

"Did he mean all of us or just you two?" Ariana asked, smiling.

"Pretty sure when he said, '*the guys* and I were heading out to break-fast, do you and *the girls* wanna join' he definitely means all of us," Hal replied, smiling back.

"Alright, I guess," Ariana said with a shrug, "but," she grinned, "we could make it just the two of you."

"As much as that sounds great, let's not," Hal responded. She really needed all of her friends with her, considering they were the only ones keeping her from sobbing even if they didn't know that.

"Are you going to respond?" Nicole asked, seeing that Hal had yet to type.

"Oh, right" Hal responded before quickly tapping a response up. She stood up, "Alright, let's go meet them."

They went and met up with the boys in the restaurant that was in the hotel. They all got a table near a window and sat down. It was a gorgeous view. The sun was turning the rock in the canyon to shades of reds and purples. While they waited for their food, they chatted.

"So," Chris started, "I know this is gonna sound crazy, but I swear I saw Shimmer last night."

"I didn't think she came up this far," Nicole said.

"Is that why you were up late?" Brad asked.

"No, I couldn't sleep," Chris then took out his phone, "See, I took a picture."

The picture was a little blurry, but it was definitely Shimmer. Hal stayed quiet and sipped her drink. She really didn't want to remember last night. She kept her eyes trained on the table.

"Hal? You're the resident expert on superheroes, does this look like her?" Chris asked. Hal looked up from the table and to Chris. He handed his phone to her, and she gently took it in her hands before looking at the photo.

That's a pretty good photo. See if you can get a copy. Roman said. She knew he could see things, but this was maybe too far.

Hal bit her lip then carded a hand through her hair before speaking, "Yeah that's Shimmer."

"See guys, I told you," Chris said. She handed his phone back to him.

"Hey, that's a really good picture of her too, can you send me a copy?" Hal asked. Chris smiled and felt a blush creep up on his face.

"Uh," Chris cleared his throat and nodded, "yeah, I can."

Their waitress then brought over their food, and they continued chatting. Chris was still blushing over the fact that Hal complimented him on his picture of Shimmer. However, he couldn't help the worry he felt when he looked at her. He saw how upset she looked, and he wanted to help her.

Hal barely touched her food. Chris and Nicole shared a look and a text conversation about how they were going to both talk to Hal and see what had been bothering her. They both knew that she wasn't herself and they wanted to help. If only they knew.

They all decided they would do some sightseeing that day around the canyon. Ariana had really bonded with Brad and William. They were both very kind to her and she really appreciated that. While they were off taking some more pictures, Nicole and Chris went into their plan of getting Hal to open up to them. So, Nicole found a snack stand and left to get water, leaving Hal alone with Chris. Nicole figured that maybe Hal would open up to Chris. She knew that the two had deep conversations and it seemed like a good idea to leave them alone for a bit. Besides, if Hal didn't open up to Chris, it was going to be Nicole's turn.

"Hey, Hal?" Chris asked, taking her attention away from the canyon. She looked at him, her blue eyes filled with sadness. She feigned a smile, though.

"Yeah?" She replied, her voice even came off happy. Hal had been trying her best all day to fake being happy.

"Ever since this morning, you've been off, are you okay?" He asked her gently. Hal blinked back tears. She didn't know how to respond. It was obvious that she wasn't okay, and she didn't know how long she could say it was because of Jeff's death.

"I had a terrible nightmare last night about Jeff's death," she lied. "It was just so... gruesome."

"It was," Chris replied, "but we're here for you, if you need anything, we're here."

"Thank you," Hal smiled.

"Of course," Chris smiled back. Hal wiped away some tears that had fallen. Chris looked at her with concern, "Want a hug?"

Hal bit her lip and nodded. He pulled her into a hug. She felt safe in his arms and a little bit more at ease. He rubbed her back a little as they embraced. Nicole cleared her throat when she approached them, causing the two to separate. Chris and Hal each had a blush creeping across their faces. Ariana, Brad, and William had also made their way back over.

"I got us all some water," Nicole said as she passed out the water bottles. Everyone gave her a 'Thank you.'

"So, what do we want to do next?" Brad asked. They all shared a look.

"We could do the skywalk," William suggested.

"Yeah! I've heard it's really cool," Ariana replied with a smile.

"That's the glass bridge, right?" Chris asked. Hal's eyes widened at his comment. She didn't want to go on that.

"Yeah, let's do it," Nicole said, "Hal, you in?"

"Yeah, sure," Hal replied with a small smile. They all went to the skywalk and took a lot of pictures. Hal almost forgot about what happened. Almost.

Later, it was Nicole's turn to get Hal alone. Chris had relayed what happened to Nicole, but they felt that Hal hadn't truly opened up. They both knew she was still off. Chris felt bad that he didn't get her to open up, but Nicole told him that it wasn't his fault. She also told him that Hal might not even open up to her. And that scared Nicole deeply.

Nicole had finally pulled Hal off to the side. It finally clicked in Hal; they were trying to get her to tell them about what was going on. Hal knew she couldn't, though. If Esimed found them and- well the worst wasn't something she could bring herself to think about. Especially considering that the worst could come to fruition now that Esimed had the stone.

"Hal, please tell me what's going on," Nicole said gently, "I know you're hurting, please let me help."

"I wish I could," Hal said as tears pricked at her eyes. She really wanted to tell her best friend everything, but she couldn't tell her. She knew that Esimed would try to hurt Nicole intentionally if Nicole knew.

"Yes you can, why would you think otherwise?" Nicole said. She looked at Hal with so much concern in her eyes. She knew her best friend was hurting, and she wanted to help. Hal bit her lip and looked at Nicole. She didn't even know what lie she could tell her. Nicole's features softened and she spoke, "Are you experiencing some depression?"

Hal nodded as tears fell from her face. Nicole quickly pulled her into a hug. Hal hated this web of lies she was getting herself into and she wanted out so badly.

-

13

The rest of their stay at the Grand Canyon was fine. Esimed didn't show up and Shimmer wasn't needed so, Hal did her best to have a good time. They had made it back home safely, too. Currently, they all were saying their goodbyes to each other in the driveway of Hal and Nicole's home. Chris and Hal were chatting at the trunk of Nicole's car. Hal smiled at something Chris said and she tucked some hair behind her ear.

"That was a much-needed getaway," Chris said. His hand subconsciously brushed against hers and she blushed.

"Yes it was," Hal replied and smiled, "Thank you for joining us. It was a lot of fun."

"Of course, thank you for letting us tag along," Chris smiled back. Then he remembered something, "Oh, there was some-"

"Chris!" William shouted, "Are you about ready?"

"I guess I better get going," Chris said, "I'll see you at work?"

"Yeah, see you at work," Hal replied. They then shared a hug before he left. Hal watched him drive off with William and Brad. She wondered what he was going to tell her before William got his attention. She figured he would tell her later.

Hal and Nicole then said goodbye to Ariana and watched her drive off. After everyone was gone, they started to take their bags into the house. Once they put their bags in their rooms, they both sat on the couch and relaxed. They sat in silence for a bit since they were both exhausted. They sat like that for almost an hour until Hal let out a sigh.

"And you're sure you're okay?" Nicole asked.

"Yeah," Hal replied. She did have the whole Esimed situation bothering her, but she couldn't talk about *that* with Nicole. Hal continued, "I'm gonna go unpack my bags, okay?"

"Okay," Nicole replied, "while you do that, I'll be in the shower."

They both stood from the couch and made their way to their rooms. Hal shut her door and started to unpack. She tried to focus on her tasks at hand; put the dirty clothes in the hamper, put the clean clothes away, put the medication on the nightstand, and so on. She had to focus on these tasks because, if she didn't, she would think about what happened and how she failed. Hal took a deep breath, clean clothes got put away, brush went on vanity, and toiletries went in her bathroom. Soon enough, she finished unpacking and put her bags away.

I have some good news.

"Oh? What is it?" Hal asked as she sat on her bed. She then laid back and folded her hands on her stomach.

I found out when Esimed is going to use the stone.

Hal sat up, "You did?"

The stone needs to be activated on the day of the solstice, which is in a week. I can help train you some more during that time.

"Yeah, we need a plan, too," she said, "I don't want to kill him. You said there was a way I could put him in an alternate dimension?"

Yes. I can do some digging, Eliana talked about doing those types of spells. I'm sure she wrote it down somewhere.

"You kept her notes?" She asked, a small smile formed on her lips.

Yes?

"That's sweet," She replied, "Roman? I need to tell you something."

What is it?

"Back when Esimed captured me, I was covered- surrounded by lightning. Is that something that has happened before?" Hal asked.

I've never seen it, but I know it's possible for you to access it. It's extra power that you have, but from what I read, it can drain you completely. Be careful when you do it.

"But *how* do I access it willingly? Last time, it just happened," she explained.

We'll work on that. Maybe tomorrow you can train? Only if you're able to take off work.

"I should be able to take tomorrow off," Hal said.

*****

The next day came, and Hal forced herself out of bed. She wanted to stay in bed and hide away from the world. She still felt like a failure because she didn't stop Esimed from getting the stone. She started to think about the worst things that could happen if she didn't defeat Esimed. She sat on her bed with tears running down her face. What was she going to do?

"Hal?" Nicole said as she knocked on the door. Hal wiped away her tears and looked at her. Nicole gave her a sympathetic look before sitting with her on the bed. Nicole spoke gently, "Are you sure you're okay?"

"Yeah," Hal said, "But I think I'm going to take today off of work."

"I think that's a great idea," Nicole said, "I'm gonna finish getting ready for work and then head out. Text me if you need anything."

"I will, thank you," Hal said. The two then shared a hug before Nicole left the bedroom.

Hal waited and listened until Nicole was out the door. Once she was gone, Hal got to work. She grabbed her band and transformed before heading off to the lake that she had been using for practice.

So, you had accessed stronger lightning? Were there any other differences? Roman said as Hal went through her basics.

"Yeah, but to be fair I was under a lot of emotional stress at the time," she responded. She paused and thought, "Well, I know I felt a surge of energy, but I don't know if anything was more powerful."

I don't want to put you through anything like that to access it. I looked through Eliana's notes and she never elaborated on it. Roman sighed as he looked through the notes again.

"Weird. Well, how do I send Esimed to another dimension?" Hal said.

We would send him to pocket dimension where authorities from my time can take him into custody. From what I've read you need to make a circle with both hands to create the portal. The portal would appear a few feet in front of you, all you have to do is push through. To close it, you do the same motion but snap at the end.

"Shouldn't be hard," Hal said. She practiced the motion until a portal appeared in front of her. She smiled when she was able to do it. Finally, she did something right.

-

14

The week Hal spent training went by fast for her. Before she knew it, it was the day before the solstice. Hal had yet to move from her bed, her nerves were going haywire, and she was terrified. Questions about the worst outcome kept crossing her mind. She called out of work because she needed to do more training. She didn't feel ready yet. Deep down, she knew she would never be fully ready, but she had to try her best.

She had gotten into the routine of stretching in the morning over the last week. She found that it helped her with being Shimmer and soothed her mind. Nicole had an early shift and left before Hal got up. She wanted to give Nicole a heads up, but she knew that could lead into her revealing herself as Shimmer. Hal sighed and finished her stretching then went to eat breakfast. Once she was done going through her morning routine, she figured it was time to train.

Are you going to train more? Haley, you'll beat Esimed, I know it. Roman said. He was worried about her even though he had faith in her. He was mostly worried about her anxiety and anything that could go wrong. He would never admit his fears to her, though.

"Thank you but I have to train more. I need to be ready if he attacks early," Hal said while holding back tears at the end. Roman wished he could be there in person to reassure her, but he couldn't risk getting her killed because of him.

I understand.

Hal transformed and flew to the lake where she had been practicing. She needed to be ready for anything that would happen.

****

Nothing happened the rest of the day and Hal went to bed late. She had been up with thoughts of worry going through her head almost non-stop until she fell asleep. When she did sleep, she had nightmares of her failing everyone. She woke up with her cheeks still wet from crying. She couldn't fail, she had to stop Esimed.

She had called out of work again to be ready for when Esimed attacked. She had her scanner app running as she paced her room, ready to transform. She was nervous about the inevitable fight coming and had already taken an anti-panic attack pill. She was still freaking out but worked on her calm down routine to ease herself a little bit. Then, she started to tell herself reassurances that she could do it and slowly became more confident.

It was a few hours until sunset and still nothing had happened. Hal was just about to ask Roman to do a scan to see if Esimed was still there when she felt a surge of energy that she had never felt before. She looked around wondering what could've caused it. Then, her scanner app went off saying there was an attack downtown.

It's him, Hal. He's attacking people with the seekers.

Hal's mouth suddenly went dry, and she felt her heart beat faster. It was real now; everything had been leading to this. She swallowed the lump in her throat and transformed before flying to the downtown area. When she got there, Esimed was floating above the convention center and looking for her. His seekers had been attacking people and looking for her. Hal flew over to float in front of him. He smirked when he saw her.

"Shimmer, glad to see you showed up. I knew attacking the people would get you to come out," he said.

"Make the seekers stop, you clearly want me," Hal said.

"Okay," he said with a snap of his fingers. Hal took a breath and noticed the stone around his neck. He saw her glance and looked at her, "Yes, this is the sunset stone and yes, I've already done the ritual. I'm too powerful for you. You should give up."

"I won't," she said before blasting an energy beam at him. She could feel her hands threatening to start shaking as the adrenaline started to pump through her veins.

Esimed stopped the energy beam in its tracks and threw it back at her. He flew to her and grabbed her by the collar and flew her down to the baseball field. He flew her into the ground as she hit his arms. He was too powerful, and she was now doubting if she could even take him on. But she had to do her best for everyone in the city and beyond. Lightning started to surround her arms and she shocked him off of her. She flew up out of the stadium, making him follow her. Once they were high enough, she shot more blue-white energy beams and lightning at him. He managed to block most of them with his own orange lightning and energy beams.

He formed a big orange energy ball that sparked off lightning. Hal felt dread as she watched him throw it at her. She threw her hands up to block it out of habit. Then, it hit her. Suddenly, her eyes started to glow while little bolts of lightning shot out of her eyes. She held the energy ball in her hands and Esimed felt terror run through him.

Hal blasted him with the energy ball he threw at her before she flew over to him. He reeled back and was briefly blinded. Hal took the opportunity to grab the sunset stone off of him. Before she could fly away from him, he flew her to the ground again. Her eyes stopped glowing and she panicked. When her back met the ground, the stone flew out of her hand and shattered.

"No!" Esimed shouted as he ran over to the stone. He felt the power drain from him while he tried to put the stone together.

Hal had managed to get up and start casting her portal spell. It was finally over; she could send him where he had to go. Her hands shook a bit as she walked over to him and pulled him to his feet.

"You're done, Esimed," she said before shoving him into the portal. Then, she quickly closed it before he could escape.

She looked over at the stone and it started to rebuild itself as the sun finished setting. The stone floated and she held out her hands for it. The stone rested in her hands as if to say thank you before disappearing. Then, Hal heard people clapping and she looked around.

"Thank you, Shimmer!" One person shouted. Then, they all started to cheer for her. Hal smiled and fought back tears as she realized that she had done it. She won.

-

15

It had been a week since Esimed was defeated. Roman had updated her that he was taken into custody. Now, Hal was wondering what Roman looked like and if he was even real. This whole time it had felt like she was living in a dream. If she saw Roman, she figured that maybe it would all be real. She sat up on her bed and figured it was now or never to ask to see him.

"You know, now that Esimed is gone, will I ever get to meet you face to face?" Hal said.

Suddenly a white light appeared in her room and Hal got up to stand in front of it. The light formed into the shape of a person and when it disappeared, there was a man standing there. He had shoulder length brown hair pulled into a half up style, brown eyes, and light warm toned skin. He was muscular and wore a black long-sleeved shirt and black pants. Hal raised a brow at him.

"Roman?" Hal asked. He nodded. She smiled, "So you are real."

"Of course, I'm real," Roman said with a concerning look on his face, "Why would you think otherwise?"

"You've always been a voice inside my head," Hal said. They looked each other over as they stood in front of each other. They both couldn't believe that they were really standing face to face with the other. It was a surreal experience. Hal then glanced into his eyes, "So, it was hard to believe that you were real."

"I'm sure that it's been a lot to take in," Roman said, "Do you want to talk about it?"

"Yes, please," Hal said.

He smiled with a nod before they moved to sit on her bed. She told him everything with how she was feeling, and he listened to her intently. He offered her comfort and encouragement when she needed it. Hal was so grateful that she could finally talk to someone face to face about being Shimmer. It had been hard to keep everything to herself. Now, she had Roman to help her.

www.ingramcontent.com/pod-product-compliance
Lightning Source LLC
Chambersburg PA
CBHW020340010826
48970CB00012B/2475